Manipulation

Manipulation

Roy Glenn

www.urbanbooks.net

Urban Books, LLC
300 Farmingdale Road, NY-Route 109
Farmingdale, NY 11735

To the extent that the image or images on the cover of this book depict a person or persons, such person or persons are merely models, and are not intended to portray any character or characters featured in the book.

ISBN 13: 978-1-64556-482-9

First Mass Market Printing August 2023
First Trade Paperback Printing April 2022
Printed in the United States of America

10 9 8 7 6 5 4 3 2 1

This is a work of fiction. Any references or similarities to actual events, real people, living or dead, or to real locales are intended to give the novel a sense of reality. Any similarity in other names, characters, places, and incidents is entirely coincidental.

Distributed by Kensington Publishing Corp.
Submit Orders to:
Customer Service
400 Hahn Road
Westminster, MD 21157-4627
Phone: 1-800-733-3000
Fax: 1-800-659-2436

Manipulation

Roy Glenn

Carpe Diem

Chapter One

John looked over at Elizabeth's thighs as he drove, thinking, *Yeah, I'm living between those thighs tonight.* He smiled at her, and she smiled back, looking at the dick print sitting noticeably on his left thigh and wondering, *Can I take all of it without gagging?*

"What?" he asked.

"Nothing," she said, but her curiosity had gotten the better of her. Therefore, Elizabeth simply leaned over and began pulling down the zipper on his pants.

"What are you doing?"

"Just drive."

As John kept his eyes on the road, Elizabeth released his dick from his pants and began to stroke it up and down slowly as it got harder in her hand.

It's pretty big, she thought as she lowered her head and took him into her wet mouth. It took a bit to adjust to the sheer size and width of it, but soon, Elizabeth was taking all of him in and hadn't gagged once.

John's eyes were wide open, and he was gripping the steering wheel tight as Elizabeth did magic with her lips, her tongue, and her right hand. Her skills were extraordinary, and he couldn't wait another second to be inside her. John rounded the next corner and drove until he found a dark place to park the car. Then he slammed the car in park.

"Get out," John said calmly. He got out and walked around to the passenger side. By the time he reached the other side of the car, she was out, had reclined the seat, and was stepping out of her panties.

"Hold these for me, please," she said, putting them into his mouth as he pulled down his pants and got in. Elizabeth pulled up her skirt around her waist and climbed in, closing the door with one hand and then guiding him inside her wetness with the other.

Once she had adjusted to the sheer size and width of it, Elizabeth began bringing it down on John hard and fast. And he loved every second of it—until they were both startled by the sound of a body crashing on the windshield!

Chapter Two

When homicide detectives Diane Mitchell and Jack Harmon arrived on the scene, they looked at the covered body on the windshield and then up at the building.

"That's a long way to fall," Jack said as he pulled back the sheet and looked at the body.

"You know what they say," Diane said.

"What's that?"

"It's not the fall; it's the sudden impact at the end that kills you." Having said that, she turned to go inside the building. "What floor are we on?"

"We're on twenty," Jack said as he pressed the button for the elevator.

"You're right. That was a long way to fall."

Diane pointed in Jack's face. "Don't say it."

"Because you know I was about to say that it's not the fall; it's the sudden impact," he chuckled as the elevator arrived, and they headed up to the twentieth floor.

Jack and Diane had been partners for years, and each had always enjoyed the witty, sometimes cutting banter that existed between them. However, their partnership took an unexpected turn while they were investigating the cold case murder of Afra Dean, a murder that Rain Robinson was accused of committing at the request of Mike Black.

One night, they were talking about the case when Diane thought, *What the hell.*

"I have a little confession to make."

She told Jack that she used to fantasize about him bending her over the hood of a car while they were on a stakeout and fucking her from behind while she looked through binoculars. She went on to explain that she had always been interested in him, but when they first became partners, Jack was just coming off a suspension for the use of excessive force, and he had a drinking problem. However, over the years, Diane had watched Jack work hard to turn all that around. Finally, he became a man that had it all together, one she could respect. Not one that a woman turned into a blackout drunk, and another used and made a fool of.

Jack smiled because he felt the same way about her. "You've been my fantasy lover since the day the lieutenant introduced us."

Jack told her that he thought it would ruin their partnership, and since he loved being her partner, he decided and chose the safe option. At Diane's encouragement, Jack shared one of his cherished fantasies and felt himself getting harder over the possibility that his long-held fantasy was about to come true. He told her that while they had a drink together after a long day. "And . . . well . . . this happens," Jack said, leaning forward and kissed Diane's lips gently.

When the elevator opened, Diane looked at the man that she was in love with. Jack was still a work in progress, but he was more like the man she thought he could be.

As they entered the apartment, they saw the crime scene technicians were busy collecting evidence, dusting for fingerprints, and capturing images of each room.

"Jack, Diane," Sergeant Hill, the supervising officer, said when he saw them come into the unit.

"What you got?" Jack asked as both he and Diane put on their gloves.

"You saw most of the story on the way in," he said and led them into another room that was used as an office with a sliding glass door that led to a balcony.

When the detectives entered the room, Jack and Diane saw there were signs of a struggle. The items that had been on the desk, Colton's desktop computer, the phone, pictures, and the lamp, were all on the floor. A bookcase was turned over, and books now covered the floor as well. And the glass door that led to the balcony was broken.

"Our working theory at this point is that there was a fight," Hill said, pointing to the items that were once on the desk but were now scattered on the floor.

"Must have been quite a fight," Diane said as she looked around the room.

"It spilled out on the balcony, and, as I said, you saw the rest of the story on your way in."

"I don't see a lot of blood." Jack looked around. "All the same, check with the hospitals nearby. See if anybody came in looking like they just left a fight club."

"I got uniforms on that as we speak," Hill informed them.

"Any ID on the victim?" Diane asked.

"Victim's name is Elias Colton."

"Witnesses?"

"We're doing a canvas of the building. So far, we got nada. The security guard said that Colton didn't have any visitors tonight, and he didn't see or notice anything or anybody out of the ordinary. We're in the process of looking for cameras that might have picked up our killer either coming or going."

"What about cameras in the building?" Jack asked.

"Malfunctioned."

"Convenient or manipulated?" Diane questioned.

"Building security said that earlier this evening, some of the cameras in the building, including the lobby, went out. He reported it to his supervisor, who promised to have somebody out here in the morning to fix it. That's him over there in the blue blazer."

"You talk to him?" Jack asked.

"I did."

"And?"

"He said he'll have someone out to fix it in the morning." Hill shrugged his shoulders and walked away.

"In the meantime, that leaves us with nothing," Diane said as she and Jack followed Hill out of the room.

"You wouldn't want it to be easy, would you? Where's the fun in that?" Jack asked.

"It would have been nice to take the elevator down to the security office and see the killer walk through the lobby covered in blood and looking at the camera," she said as they began looking around the unit.

"No forced entry. So, we know that Colton knew his killer," Jack said.

"Agreed," Diane said, pointing to the glass on the coffee table. "That second circle from a glass suggested that Colton knew the killer well enough to have a drink."

"But the signs of the struggle are in the office, which suggests that the fight occurred over something in *that* room. Probably over some business between them."

"Enough to kill for," Diane said.

Chapter Three

"You're pregnant. Congratulations," Daniella had said excitedly on the day that Rain came to see her at the office. "Or not?" she added nervously when she saw the look on Rain's face.

After leaving Perry's Mount Vernon doctor's office, Rain drove around thinking about what she would do. Daniella Ramsey had just told her that she was pregnant. She never even thought about having a baby. Although she loved kids, Rain loved *other people's* kids when they came to visit her.

But then the little fuckers need to go home.

It was all so surreal to Rain. Daniella showed her the first image of her baby: a white blip on the screen. Rain never wanted children. Therefore, being pregnant was unfathomable for her.

Rain thought about all the things that she'd heard that pregnant women should and shouldn't do: Don't drink alcohol, don't smoke, don't do drugs, eat healthily, don't take any medicines without first talking to your doctor, get plenty of rest, and exercise. It all seemed overwhelming.

Pregnant?
A baby inside of me?
A mother?
What about my job?
How am I going to tell Carter?

After a long string of disastrous relationships, Rain had come to believe that finding Mr. Right and settling down with the perfect man wasn't in the cards for her. Therefore, she was perfectly content to deal with Mr. Right now, and Carter Garrison played that part so well. Nobody had fucked her the way that he had since Nick had had enough of her shit.

Rain thought about her relationship with Nick. He was married to April, and they were happy, happier than he ever was when they were together. She had to admit that she was jealous of what the two of them shared. It always made her wonder why it couldn't have worked between the two of them. The answer was simple, however.

"Me. That's the difference: me. *I* was the problem. *I* was the reason it didn't work."

After Nick's leaving devastated her, Rain bounced from man to man as long as they could satisfy her immense sexual appetite. Then she would throw them away when she was done with them. And then came Carter Garrison. She wanted him to bend her over and dick her down from the first time she saw him. But even though he satisfied her desires and fucked her the way she wanted to be fucked, Rain could list many reasons why Carter wasn't Mr. Right for her. She laughed.

"He got a big dick, and men with big dicks know they have a big dick and feel like they need to share that dick with every woman they see." And *that* was Carter Garrison.

This wasn't really happening to her. There was a life growing inside of her. This was not supposed to happen to her, and this was not how she thought she would feel about it.

Eventually, Rain arrived at J.R.'s and made her way through the early evening Saturday night crowd to the stairs leading to her office.

"What's up, Chelsea?"

"Hey, Rain. Carter's been looking for you?"

"I know," Rain said because she'd been ignoring his calls all day and went into her office.

"He wants you to call—" Chelsea said to the slamming door.

When Rain closed the door, Chelsea immediately picked up the phone and called Carter at Romans, the pizzeria/sports-betting operation.

"What's up, Chelsea?"

"Rain's here."

"You tell her that I said to call me?"

"I did."

"What she say?"

"She closed the door."

"Figures." He paused and thought for a second or two. "I'm on my way there. Let me know if she leaves."

"Will do," Chelsea said, ending the call, and then she stood up.

Chelsea took a different approach, unlike Yarissa, who wore jeans and a different J.R.'s T-shirt to the club just about every night. She saw the job as Rain's receptionist and personal valet through Mileena's and Demi's eyes. Each of them had gone from having that job to floor manager to being the club manager. Now that Mileena had moved on, Demi was the club manager. To Chelsea, she was on that same career path to management. Therefore, she dressed for the job that she wanted and not the job that she had. That night, Chelsea was dressed head to toe in Kate Spade New York.

Alwan and Ricky, Rain's bodyguards, came up the stairs in time to catch a glimpse of Chelsea in the midnight-blue, tight-fitting design of the round neck, sleeveless dress with intricate cut-out detail at the neck and hemline. She wore white satin pumps on her feet as she tapped on Rain's door and stepped inside to speak to Rain.

Ricky shook his head and sat down. "Yarissa was fine, but damn, that muthafucka is *bad*."

Alwan shook his head. "You say that about every woman you see." He laughed. "You wouldn't know a bad muthafucka if you tripped over her."

"Whatever, nigga. I know that is one *bad* mutha-fucka," Ricky said, pointing at the door to Rain's office.

Once inside the office, Chelsea looked at Rain as Rain unholstered her guns and took off her vest. She was still new to the job and feeling her way through with Rain, but the look on Rain's face said, *Don't say a fuckin' word to me,* so she didn't.

So Chelsea did what she always did when Rain arrived in her office. She had gone to the bar, picked up the bottle of Patrón, and was about to pour when Rain finally noticed that she was in the office.

"What are you doing?"

Chelsea froze and paused to think if that was a trick question. "Pouring you a drink," she said slowly, and Rain's mind flashed back to her conversation with Daniella.

"I need a fuckin' drink," she said after finding out that she was pregnant.

"Well, the usual message to pregnant women is don't drink any alcohol because it can cause major problems for the pregnant woman and her baby. However, there's a study published in the Journal of Obstetrics and Gynecology *that says minimal alcohol use during the first trimester doesn't appear to increase the risk of complications as previously believed,"* was what Daniella told her.

Rain considered those words for a second or two before she said, "Go ahead," and sat down as Chelsea poured her drink and then brought it to her. "You can go now."

Chelsea walked to the door and was about to reach for the handle but stopped before she opened it.

"Are you all right, Rain?"

"No."

"Anything I can do?"

"No," Rain said and picked up the glass. "But thanks for giving a fuck enough to ask." Then she put the glass down without drinking any of it.

"I'm here if you need me," she said and left the office and Rain to her thoughts.

Damn.

That was the word that kept rolling around in her mind.

Damn.

Rain didn't really want a baby, nor was she interested in experiencing everything that came with it.

Damn.

There was no wave of joy about her being a mother. Instead, she just sat there feeling slightly numb about the life-changing news she'd just heard. Rain was pregnant.

With a real live baby.

Something about that just don't sound right.

As she sat there, she played around with the idea of not telling anyone for a couple of days, especially not Carter.

After all, tests could be wrong, right?

But the idea of not telling anyone, especially Carter, ended when he burst through the door and demanded to know, "What the fuck is going on with you?" he shouted and slammed the door behind him.

"I'm fuckin' pregnant—*that's* what's fuckin' going on with me," Rain shouted back, and Carter looked shocked.

"What?"

"You fuckin' heard me, muthafucka. I'm fuckin' pregnant—that's what's fuckin' going on with me!" she shouted again.

Carter didn't say anything for a second or two, and then he went and plopped down on the couch. "Pregnant?" He immediately stood up and went to the bar.

"Pregnant."

For a second or two, he thought about asking her who the father was, but the daggers that were blasting from her eyes told him that it would be a bad idea. He had seen Rain's fury unleashed, and he wanted no part of it.

"I need a drink." Carter picked up a bottle of Hennessy Black.

Rain drained her glass. "Pour me one too."

Carter stopped, put down the bottle, and looked at Rain. "Should you be drinking . . . you know . . . being pregnant and shit?"

"Daniella Ramsey said that a little drink ain't gonna kill me."

Carter chuckled as he picked up the bottle of Patrón. "Daniella Ramsey said that?"

"She made the shit sound all medical and quoted a fuckin' article, but, yeah, nigga, that's what the fuck she said," Rain barked as Carter came around the bar and handed her a drink.

"You gonna have it?"

"You *want* me to have it?"

"No."

"I knew it."

"I think you should have an abortion."

"I knew you were gonna say that too."

Rain finished her drink and stood up. She was about to go to the bar and pour another one, but in that second, *Don't drink alcohol, don't smoke, don't do drugs . . .*

Maybe I had enough to drink, she thought and set the glass on the bar.

"But I'm thinking about having it," she said, and, yes, there was a part of her that could not believe that she had just said that out loud.

"Seriously?"

"Seriously. What's so wrong about that?"

"Nothing . . . I guess. I mean, it's just not something I thought you were interested in."

"Me either," she said and sat down without pouring herself a drink.

"I mean, I've heard you say, more than once, that you have no maternal instincts." Carter paused. "Not to mention that you are the boss of this Family."

"I know. Both of those are true, but I'm still thinking about having it."

"I'm not ready to be a father, Rain," Carter said.

"I know. But this ain't about you." She paused and then glared at Carter. "And how your arrogant ass know that you're the father?"

"Am I?"

"Yeah, muthafucka, you're the father."

"I was just asking because we always used a condom."

"Except that *one* time at Romans," Rain said, and Carter immediately recalled it all.

Don't you wanna . . . he could hear her saying that night outside of Romans. Carter smiled when he thought about how hot they were for each other in those days.

Come on.

He remembered grabbing her by the hand and fast walking her in Romans. He was so anxious to get to her that night because Rain's sex had him completely blown, and he couldn't get enough of her.

As they made their way to the office, instead of speaking to everybody, Carter wanted to tell them to get the fuck out because they were the boss and underboss of The Family, and they had come there to fuck—not talk.

The second they were in the office and had locked the door, they stripped each other down, and Rain grabbed his tie.

You need to gag my ass, Carter remembered Rain saying before she bent over the desk, and he slammed his entire dick in her because that was the way she liked it . . . grabbing her shoulders and pulling her to him and slamming his entire length in her as hard as she could stand it. And, yes, Rain could take some dick.

And when she spun around, dropped to her knees, pulled down the gag, and took him into her mouth, Carter thought that he would lose it right there. Fuckin' Rain was so fuckin' hot, and watching her take his dick deeper and deeper in and out of her mouth, moaning and fingering herself while she sucked . . .

Damn.

He loved fuckin' Rain Robinson.

He was losing his mind over that insane pussy. Damn right, he remembered that night . . . Rain putting the gag back in her mouth, hopping up on the desk, and he slammed it in her again. Carter closed his eyes for a second or two. He could see and almost feel their bodies slamming violently into each other, her eyes opening wide when she felt him swelling inside her, and they came hard together . . . but without a condom.

Carter shook his head and thought about it. He needed to stay calm and not overreact. But like Rain, he was overwhelmed by the sudden news that he would be a father. While he was with Mileena, he was excited when she said she wanted to have his baby. But when they broke up, Carter felt like his chance to be a father had ended when she closed her car door and drove away. He had to admit that he was worried, a little scared, even because he wasn't ready to be a father. Carter thought that the best thing for him to do at this point was to listen to her. He would have to support Rain and help her decide what was best for her and the baby. Because like she said, it wasn't about him.

"I think this is something we need to talk about," he said, and Rain looked at him like he was a fool.

"Why? What's to talk about? You already told me what you think I should do, so you tell me, what we got to talk about?" Rain asked as her phone began ringing.

Carter said nothing.

"That's what I thought," she said and swiped talk. "This Rain."

"Hey, Lorraine, it's Millie."

"Hey, Millie, what's up?"

"When you get a chance, stop by. There's something that I want to talk to you about."

"Is everything all right?"

"Yes, Lorraine, everything is fine. There's just something I need to talk to you about."

"Okay, Millie. I'll be through there," Rain said and ended the call. "That was Millie."

"What she want?"

Rain stood up and put on her vest. "She didn't say."

"Want me to come with you?" he asked because he still felt like they should talk. And besides, they were going to have a baby together.

"No. I need some time to be alone and think," she said, putting on her vest and then holstering her guns. "I'll get with you tomorrow," Rain told him, walking toward the door.

Alwan and Ricky bounced up when the office door opened. "Let's go," she said, and they fell in behind her.

Chapter Four

"Where you going?" Rain asked Ricky as he drove.

"Going to Millie's," he said.

"We ain't going to Millie's. That was just some shit I said to get away from Carter."

"Where you want to go then?" Alwan asked.

"I don't know. Just drive."

"You heard the woman. Drive," Alwan said.

Rain looked at Alwan, nodded her head, and settled into her seat. She had come to respect Alwan, even like him, and that wasn't always the case. He had been her bodyguard for the last four years, a job he earned by being the last man standing, or driving, as it was in this particular case. Her previous two bodyguards, which, by the way, she only had because Black insisted that she needed one, Omari and Nelson, were killed the night that Rain was shot coming out of J.R.'s. After that, her captains sent men to protect her, and Alwan was one of those men. There was a captain's meeting at J.R.'s, and when it came time to take Rain and

Wanda back to her safe house, Alwan was assigned
to the Tahoe with Yarissa and Glenda.

Four Tahoes and nine men left J.R.'s that night
and were on a long stretch of road when two Chevy
Silverados came up behind the convoy and were
closing fast. One of the cars cut in front of the trail-
ing vehicle and blocked its path. Then two men
stood up in the bed of the Silverado and opened
fire on the Tahoe with heavy weapons, killing the
three occupants as they tried to exit the vehicle.

"We're gonna end up shooting our way out of
this," Wanda said and handed Rain a Heckler &
Koch MP7A1.

"I know," Rain said, and they did.

The vehicle with Glenda and Yarissa was
rammed, run off the road, and then flipped over
twice before landing upright on its wheels. Damon,
who was driving the Tahoe, was killed, but Alwan
survived, got out of the vehicle, and got in the firefight that ended when Rain mounted the M203
grenade launcher on her weapon and fired. The
explosion that followed took out the Silverados
and their remaining attackers. He had been Rain's
bodyguard ever since.

During the years that followed, Alwan got to not
only know but also care about Rain. To him, Rain
Robinson wasn't just the boss of The Family. She
was like his mean and bossy big sister, and he had
sworn an oath to himself that he would give his life

to protect her, a job that Rain didn't make easy for him because of her habit of sneaking away when she didn't want to be bothered or have people in her business. But now, since she was pregnant and avoiding Carter, Rain took Alwan and Ricky with her wherever she went, which was fine with him.

As for Rain, she sat in the backseat with her eyes closed, trying but not succeeding in thinking about something other than being pregnant. She could hear the sound of Carter's voice in her head. *I think this is something we need to talk about.* And maybe he was right. It was something that they should talk about, but she wasn't feeling it. Rain slammed her fist into the seat next to her.

Think of something else, damn it.

Rain thought about her position in The Family. Although Mike Black was still the actual boss of The Family, she carried the title. Since becoming a member of The Family when she all but handed J.R.'s to Nick, Rain had proven herself to be a loyal soldier. Having had the opportunity to work for Nick and then Wanda before Black first threatened to kill Rain and then took her to the next level, she considered herself lucky. When she and Black were in the streets, no one could stop them.

Those were good days, she thought—*definitely more fun.*

If she chose to be honest, she'd have to admit that she missed those days, in the spots every night, hanging out, talking shit, bustin' a few heads, and eliminating their enemies. The Family had been in a state of war practically since the day she met Nick. Bobby had once jokingly said that it was Shy's fault that they'd been on a war footing since the day she and Black met, but Rain disagreed. Although she wasn't always the cause of the trouble, you could be sure that Rain Robinson was in the middle of it. But all that was behind them now, and The Family was enjoying a rare and extended period of peace. And to be honest, Rain was bored. Now that she was boss of The Family, Rain spent most of her time at J.R.'s, either in meetings or dealing with whatever came her way.

"But why?" she said aloud.

"What you say, Rain?" Alwan asked.

"Nothing. Just thinking out loud."

But the question stood, and it was a valid one. Why was she spending every night sitting in the office at J.R.'s? *Mike Black didn't sit his ass up at Cuisine every fuckin' night. That nigga used to stay in the streets.* She laughed out loud. Alwan and Ricky looked back at her.

That is until Shy came back from the dead. Now, you can hardly get him to leave the house.

"Roll me by Dime Piece," she said, deciding that there was no reason why she couldn't make the rounds like she did in the old days. *After all, you are the boss of The Family, so who's gonna tell you no.*

"Now, we talking," Ricky said excitedly and made a U-turn.

Her first thought was to roll by Conversations and then go talk to Sherman.

Another nigga that don't want to leave the house no more.

But she always talked to them. And when she did leave J.R.'s, most times it was Conversations where she went.

Fuck that.

Dime Piece, the strip club that once belonged to DP before Rain ended him, was now run by Chee-Chee. She used to hang out with Shy and Ryder. They were the Deadly Three back in the day until Shy went to college, Ryder moved to the West Coast, and Chee-Chee went to jail for armed robbery. She also ran the online video chat rooms where women provided entertainment for their clients' enjoyment. They belonged to DP too, you know, before Rain killed him, and she gave them both to Ryder to run.

When Ricky parked the car, Alwan opened the door for Rain, and she went inside. It didn't take long before Chee-Chee was alerted that she was in the club. After checking the monitors, Chee-Chee picked up her phone and called Ryder.

"What she doing there?" she asked because Rain hadn't been there since the day they took over the spot.

"I haven't been out there to see."

"What she doing?"

"She sitting at the bar."

"Who's with her?"

"Alwan and Ricky."

Ryder thought for a second or two. "Okay. Let me know what she wants."

"You got it," Chee-Chee said and got up to go see why Rain was there because there had to be a reason.

When she opened the door to her office, Alwan was standing there.

"Rain wants to see you."

"Hello, Alwan. How are you?"

"I'm fine, Chee-Chee. Rain wants to see you." He smiled. "That better?"

"Much," she said and walked past him on her way to the bar.

Rain stood up when she saw her coming. "What's up, Chee-Chee?"

"I'm good. What's up with you?"

Rain felt like saying, *I'm fuckin' pregnant,* that's *what's up with me.* "I'm awesome. Everything quiet here?"

"As quiet as a tittie bar can be."

"Any more problems with Kojo's people?"

Kordell Jones, a.k.a. Kojo, was a low-level drug dealer that had the good fortune of getting arrested and sentenced to fifteen years for murder.

There, he met members of The Curcio Family, Johnny Boy DiLeonardo, who was serving time for a parole violation, and heroin dealer Marco Ricci. When Angelo Collette's uncle, the former head of The Curcio Family, Big Tony, wanted to have a greater presence in the market, he provided a lawyer for Kojo, who subsequently had his conviction overturned on a technicality. Johnny Boy passed on his knowledge of how to run a drug-trafficking organization to Kojo.

Big Tony's plan for taking over that market was to push the Caldwell Enterprise out of the way. He had conspired with police Deputy Inspector Cavanaugh and Dennis Allen, the assistant US Attorney for the Southern District of New York, to create a task force, headed by Lieutenant Rachael Dawkins, with the sole purpose of successfully dismantling the Caldwell Enterprise, something that Rain regretted having a part in.

Because it concerned Angelo, Black had declared Kojo and his people off-limits, but he still wanted to know everything about how they were set up, so she needed to get on top of it.

"Nope. Since Money and BC handled that one problem I was having, all the rest of them been behaving themselves."

"Any of them here tonight?"

Chee-Chee looked around the club. "I don't see any of them. They're probably in the VIP room, throwing stupid money at these little girls." She paused. "There goes one of them now," Chee-Chee said and pointed to a man coming out of the VIP room.

"Who's he?"

"Calls himself Truck. He's one of Kojo's lieutenants."

"What's up with him?"

"Him and Ryder don't get along."

"What's up with that?"

"He's cool, but as I said, he throws crazy money at the ladies, waitresses too, so he thinks he owns them." Chee-Chee paused and smiled. "So one night, Ryder was here, and she's talking to one of the waitresses, and he walks up, grabs her by the arm, and says, 'Come on, my niggas need some drinks.'"

Both Rain and Chee-Chee laughed.

"What Ryder do?" Rain asked.

"You know my girl is foolish, right? So she gets up on stage and yelled at the top of her lungs, 'Turn off the fuckin' music!'" Chee-Chee said, and she and Rain laughed some more. "Then she said, 'Now, I need every last one of you to get your asses up on this stage right fuckin' now.'"

"I know she didn't have to ask twice."

"Trust and believe all the ladies are scared to death of Ryder, so you know they all came running from all over the club." Chee-Chee paused. "Then she looks at Truck and says, 'Now, you see who runs this joint.' Truck nodded his head slowly, and Ryder told the DJ to play some music and told the ladies to dance."

"She embarrassed him," Rain said.

"It's been on ever since."

"What about Pago's? I hear they like to hang out there too."

"Same thing," Chee-Chee said. "Since Money and Baby Chris did their thing, Zach says they're no problem. Just likes to spend money."

Rain looked around for her men. Ricky was standing in front of the stage, making it rain on the dancer, while Alwan was standing nearby where he could see her and the door.

"I'm out. Tell Ryder I came through."

"Will do," Chee-Chee said, and as soon as Rain left, she called Ryder to report.

"Where do you want to go now?" Alwan asked as he opened the door for Rain.

"Take me to Pago's," she said and got in. Even though Chee-Chee said that Zack told her things were quiet, Rain wanted to see for herself. "Then roll by La Chatte. I wanna talk to Mercedes."

Rain needed information about Kojo. Although she didn't like her because she really hadn't forgiven her for fucking Nick behind her back, Mercedes was always a good source of information. *Almost as good a source as Sherman was in his prime,* she thought as Ricky started the car and headed for Pago's. *Now, the nigga don't want to leave the house.*

When Cynt was murdered, Black decided that he wanted something a bit more upscale that was designed to appeal to his more affluent clientele. So he separated the dancers from the gambling, had Jada West recruit and train the ladies, and once she had taught Mercedes how a Mike Black club was supposed to be run, she opened La Chatte.

"Honestly, Rain, this is not their type of establishment, so I can't say that I know any more about them than you do."

Rain laughed. "That's because your ladies don't get excited about a muthafucka flashing a couple of hundred-dollar bills at them."

Mercedes looked offended. "Certainly not."

Rain hung around La Chatte for a while longer before she headed out. Her next stop was The Playhouse, the club run by Barbara Ray. She didn't think that Barbara knew any more about Kojo than anybody else, but she was Bobby's daughter, and that was reason enough to check on her. Barbara told Rain that she was having problems with a drug gang called the G-40s trying to shake her down for protection money.

"Nothing I can't handle, Aunt Rain," Barbara said, and Rain knew that it was true. Despite her pampered princess upbringing, Barbara was a force that had to be taken seriously.

After that, Alwan and Ricky took Rain around to all the moneymaking spots in The Family. Going to the sites, being around her people, drinking, and talking shit instead of sitting around her office was the most fun that she'd had in years. And it was something that she planned on continuing once she resolved the whole pregnancy thing one way or the other.

It was after five in the morning when they arrived at Conversations. When Rain got to Jackie's office, Honey was just coming out. When Javan killed Glover for not retaliating when Barbara killed Spike, Honey took over at Glover's.

"What's up, Honey?" Rain said, and it startled her.

"Hey, Rain."

"Everything all right at Glover's?" Rain asked as they passed each other.

"Everything is fine," she said, even though it wasn't. Honey was too shocked that Rain even knew who she was to mention the problems she was having.

"You let me know if that changes," Rain said and closed the door before Honey could reply. "What's up, Jackie?"

"Everything is all good in my world for a change," Jackie said and thought about Honey and her issues as Rain sat down. "Well, *almost* everything."

"What's up?"

"Archie Smith and James Oliver are trying to push Honey out at Glover's."

"What's up with that?"

"They both think they deserve the spot," Jackie said. "I got Marvin and Baby Chris on it." They were Jackie's right and left hands.

"Then it's nothing for me to worry about."

Chapter Five

"Who was Elias Colton?" That was the question that Diane asked Jack to begin their investigation into his murder the following morning. "And who would want to kill him?"

"According to his profile on the company's website, Elias Colton is the owner of Titanium Distributing Service. The company was founded in 2001 by husband-and-wife team Elias and Cecilia," Jack read, scanning for any information that he considered important. "A member of the Association of Black Businesses," he paused, "with more than two hundred and fifty million in annual revenue. In addition, it says that Colton has had an extensive manufacturing background as a senior executive with both domestic and international assignments. And Colton has a bachelor of science in commerce from DePaul University and an MBA from the University of Notre Dame."

"What stuck out to me was the two hundred and fifty million in annual revenue. Money *always* says motive to me," Diane said.

"And it's usually a safe bet. Especially with *that* kind of money."

"I think that the first thing that we need to do is to establish if this was an accident, or did the killer go there intending to kill Colton?"

"I see your point, but it is a distinction without a difference. It's murder, no matter how you slice it," Jack said. "How they want to charge it is above my pay grade."

"That may be true, but it will help us to establish a motive. And the reason why may tell us who."

"So, the question is . . . Who was Elias Colton?"

Diane picked up her phone and leaned back as she continued reading from the site. "Titanium Distributing Service is a joint venture with Toyota Tsusho America Inc."

"A joint venture with Toyota. That screams money."

"I say again that two hundred and fifty million in annual revenue sticks out to me." Diane nodded. "So, yeah, I'm thinking this may just be about money."

"Isn't it always?"

"Money or sex; take your pick."

"Definitely need to talk to the wife and anyone else who is gonna gain from this. Are there any children involved?"

"One. A daughter, Megan," Diane said. "She lives in northern Colorado. She's married and has two children. Her husband's name is Homer. He's a construction site supervisor, and she works as a physician's assistant. That's where the wife was at the time of the murder, in Boulder, visiting.

"She got back to the city late last night. We'll go see her this afternoon. What else we got on Colton?"

"Not much. Just more bullshit from the corporate site. Colton has concentrated on improving the quality of life in the communities where he lives and does business. Mr. Colton firmly believes in sharing his success and encouraging other entrepreneurs, both minority and otherwise, toward achieving success in business ventures. His companies have partnered with the Minority Business Development Council and fledgling minority companies to develop business partnerships to grow their business. That kind of shit."

"We need to look into the Association of Black Businesses and its membership and this Minority Business Development Council and find out who these fledgling minority companies are and his relationship to them."

"Agreed. I say we start at Colton's office. If this was about business, and I think that it is, that's the best place to start." Diane put down her phone and saw the look on Jack's face. "What? You don't want to start at the office?"

Jack paused to think before he answered. "No, it's not that. I agree that's the best place to start."

"But . . .?"

"But we're thinking it's about money mainly because the fight occurred in the office, but what if it wasn't about business? What if the fight *was* over a personal matter?"

"Like sex?" Diane sat up. "I see your point, but it is a distinction without a difference. It's murder, no matter how you slice it," she said, and Jack smiled.

"Touché."

"But I do see your point. Whoever the killer was, Colton knew them well enough to let them in and to offer them a drink." She lay back. "That's another thing that's bothering me."

"What's that?"

"Security said that Colton had no visitors, but we know for a fact that somebody, the killer, entered the building that night sometime before nine fifty-seven."

"That bothered me too, but I think when we talk to security again, he's gonna tell us that he was away from that desk at some time before ten and didn't mention it because it will probably get him fired," Jack said, and Diane laughed.

"I'll tread lightly on that one then." She giggled. "So, here's the plan. We go to Colton's office, this afternoon we hit wifey, and then we swing by and talk to the security guard."

"That is if he's working tonight."

"True. I'll get his home address, and we drop in on him after we leave the office."

"Sounds like a plan," Jack said and paused. "You hungry?"

Diane looked at him like the answer should be obvious. "Always."

"We can grab something on the way," he said and was about to get out of bed when he saw that Diane had posted her sad face. "What?"

"I want pancakes."

"Pancakes? Really, Diane?"

"Yes, Jack, really." She sat up in bed. "I *really* do want some pancakes for breakfast."

"We don't have time for me to make pancakes for you."

"Yes, we do. It's early, and you know it doesn't take you long to make pancakes. And your pancakes are so good." She moved closer to Jack in bed and kissed him on the cheek. "Please," she cooed and kissed him again.

"And I guess you want some bacon to go with it too?"

Diane nodded. "Yes, please."

Jack smiled. "Okay, pancakes and bacon it is," he said, rolling over to kiss Diane's lips gently before he got out of bed. "But you're driving today."

"Deal. I got no problem with that whatsoever. As long as I get pancakes, I'm fine," Diane said. She got out of bed and headed to the bathroom while Jack went into the kitchen to start breakfast.

It was just after nine o'clock that morning when they arrived at the offices of Titanium Distributing Service. As expected, the office was in a somber mood following the news of the death of their visionary founder.

"Good morning, and welcome to Titanium Distributing Service. How can I help you today?" the receptionist asked.

Jack and Diane showed their badges.

"I'm Detective Harmon, and this is Detective Mitchell. We're investigating the murder of Elias Colton."

"We have an appointment to speak with a Doris Bessemer," Diane said.

"Please, have a seat. Ms. Bessemer will be with you shortly."

"Thank you," Diane said, and they went to sit and wait.

After a thirty-minute wait in the lobby looking at the framed artwork, watching people come and go about their day, Jack and Diane were escorted into the office of Doris Bessemer, Elias Colton's executive assistant. She was Cecilia's aunt and had held the position since he and Cecilia first founded the company. When they were shown into the office, Doris stood up to greet them. It was apparent to the detectives that she'd been crying.

"I apologize for keeping you waiting," she said as they shook hands.

"I understand, and I am very sorry for your loss," Diane said compassionately.

"As you can imagine, this came as quite a shock to both our family and the company."

"Once again, I am so sorry for your loss," Diane said.

"What can you tell me about Mr. Colton?" Jack wasted no time in asking.

"Elias was a great man," she began and then treated Jack and Diane to an African American success story of a man that came from a humble background. After a stint in the army, he started his business career as an entry-level accountant. He rose up the corporate ladder through hard work and dedication to found a highly successful international corporation.

"Highly successful men like Mr. Colton tend to make a lot of enemies along the way up the ladder," Diane said. "Do you know of anyone that might have had a problem with Mr. Colton?"

"No, not at all. Quite the opposite," Doris said, smiling brightly, and then she paused. "Everybody loved Mr. Colton," she said, and both Jack and Diane noticed the way her facial expression changed after she said, "everybody loved him." It was as if she thought of something that conflicted with that statement.

Jack and Diane looked at each other and then at Doris. "And you can't think of *anyone* that didn't love Mr. Colton?" Diane asked, and Doris exhaled.

"Well," she paused, "I am not the one that starts nor participates in gossip, and if Cissy knew I was telling you this, she'd be very upset."

Diane leaned forward. "I won't tell her if you don't," she said, and Jack smiled.

"I've heard some rumors."

"Rumors?" Jack questioned.

Doris leaned forward and spoke in a hushed tone. "I've heard the rumors about Elias being involved in multiple 'indiscretions.' Some of those affairs, I'm told, were with married women."

"Having multiple indiscretions with married women does tend to make enemies, Mrs. Bessemer," Jack said.

"So why don't you tell me what you know about those multiple indiscretions, and if you don't mind, start with the married ones," Diane said, and that led to a discussion about the latest woman Colton was seeing.

Her name was Gayle Eager. She and her husband, Albert, met Colton five years ago when they became members of the Association of Black Businesses. However, it was only this past year and a half that Elias began mentoring the couple in their janitorial business. The affair between Elias and Gayle started a few months later. Jack and

Diane would try to arrange interviews with them later that day.

The detectives spent the rest of the morning at Titanium talking to a random sampling of employees, and they left, sure of one thing.

"Elias Colton considered himself a lady's man," Jack said as his phone rang. "Harmon."

"What's up, Jack? It's Davenport."

"What you got for me?" Jack said to one of his more reliable snitches.

"Manny Fernandez."

"Manny Fernandez?" Jack said, and Diane's head snapped around.

"On a silver platter. You want him?"

"Hell yeah. Where is he?"

"Meet me at Fortieth and Fifth Avenue near Bryant Park in about an hour."

"We'll be there," Jack said and ended the call. "That was Tommy Davenport. He says he can give us Manny Fernandez on a silver platter. He wants us to meet him near Bryant Park in an hour."

"Then why are we sitting around here? Let's go get him," Diane said, and they left Titanium.

Manny Fernandez was a stickup artist that liked to rob jewelry stores. He got on Jack and Diane's radar when he stepped up to murder when the clerk he shot during his last robbery died. He'd been laying low for the last couple of months. Diane's sources told her that Fernandez was somewhere in South Jersey, while Jack's people said he'd gone back to Puerto Rico. It was only Davenport that said to be patient.

"He'll crawl out of his hole like the snake he is when the money runs out."

An hour later, Jack and Diane were standing on the corner of Fortieth Street and Fifth Avenue when they saw Tommy Davenport coming down the street. He was a small-time gambler: horses, cards, dice, that type of thing, but he got around, so he heard things—the kind of things that people would gladly pay to hear. Davenport didn't like the term "snitch," even though that was what he was. He considered himself an "information broker," and it didn't matter if it was a cop or criminal. He had information for a price.

"What's up, Jack?" Davenport said, then turned to Diane and bowed slightly. "Detective Mitchell," he said respectfully.

"Okay, we're here. Where's Fernandez," Diane said impatiently. It wasn't that she didn't like Davenport. He was all right as far as snitches go. But Jack was playing good cop, so it was her job to play bad cop.

Davenport looked at his watch. "Let's take a walk," he said and started walking down Fifth Avenue. Jack and Diane looked at each other and hurried to catch up.

"Where are we going?" Diane asked after they'd walked several blocks.

"It's not much farther, Detective Mitchell, I promise."

"This better turn out to be more than just a casual stroll down Fifth Avenue," Diane said, and Jack smiled at her because he enjoyed watching her bad-cop routine.

"I swear it is," Davenport said and stopped. He pointed across the street. "I present to you one Manny Fernandez."

When the detectives looked in the direction Davenport was pointing, they saw Manny Fernandez walking into Zales Jewelers.

Both Jack and Diane were reaching for their guns when Davenport said, "Relax. He's not there to rob the place. He's just checking out the inside," he said with his hand out.

"Thanks, Tommy," Jack said, put a hundred-dollar bill in his hand, and Davenport walked away without saying another word.

Jack and Diane kept their eyes on the store and waited with their fellow New Yorkers for the streetlight to change. When it did, and with their eyes still on Zales, the detectives crossed the crowded New York City street. When they reached the corner, Jack and Diane looked at all the civilians walking by the store.

"Lunchtime. A lot of people." Diane thought that the scene could get ugly quickly if he came out of the store, saw them, and started shooting. "How do you want to play this?"

"I seriously don't want to go into that store, and he starts shooting."

"Especially if he's just there to case the place."

"We need to take him when he exits the store."

"I agree."

"I'll go around to the other side of the store, and we get him in a crossfire when he comes out," Jack said, walking past the entrance. He and Diane then took positions on either side of the door and waited for Fernandez to exit. Diane peeked in the window.

"What's he doing?"

"Looking at the display cases." She moved her head back quickly. "Here he comes," she said as the detectives drew their weapons and converged on the door. The crowd of passersby scattered as Fernandez walked out of the shop.

"Manny Fernandez, you're under arrest for the murder of Joanne Phillips," Jack yelled.

Fernandez took off running right between them.

"Shit," Diane said as she and Jack pursued him.

With the detectives on his heels, Fernandez ran out into the street. He dodged some cars, which came to a screeching stop. He began running down the street along the white lines as drivers yelled and cursed him. When the cars stopped at the red light, the people watched as Fernandez stopped and grabbed the handle of a Honda Accord and yanked out the woman who was driving. She screamed and fought with everything she had. It gave Jack and Diane time to catch up. Finally, Fernandez punched the woman in the face, got in, and shut the door. Jack stuck his gun in the window just as Fernandez was about to put the car in gear.

"Don't do it."

Fernandez turned to the passenger side and saw Diane standing with her weapon pointed at him. He moved his hand slowly away from the gear shift, put up his hands, and surrendered.

Chapter Six

Once they had finished booking, processing, and questioning Manny Fernandez, it was too late to talk to Gayle Eager or her husband, Albert. Therefore, Jack and Diane went to Colton's building to speak to the security guard, Jonathan Nolan. When they arrived, unfortunately for the detectives, Nolan had the night off. So instead of calling it a night and heading home, they went up to Colton's apartment to walk the crime scene again. Jack and Diane entered the apartment and turned on the lights. Except for the items collected as evidence, everything was as it was the last time they were there.

"Where do you want to start?" Diane asked as they walked the unit.

"I think we should concentrate our focus on the office. But let's look around out here first. Maybe we'll get lucky."

"I'll take the kitchen," she said, putting on her gloves, and Jack got started looking around the living room.

She didn't find much in the kitchen. Other than beer, orange juice, and some half-eaten takeout, the refrigerator was practically empty. There were a few plates and glasses in the cabinets, and the dishwasher was empty.

"So, we know he doesn't spend a lot of time here," Diane said aloud and left the kitchen.

After looking around the living room and not finding anything, Jack moved on to the bedroom. The first thing that caught his attention was that the bed was a mess. One of the pillows, as well as the sheet, were on the floor. Next, he walked into the closet and saw three suits, five shirts, a tie rack, and four pairs of shoes on the floor.

"I see there are signs of a struggle in here too," Diane said when she entered the room and saw the bed.

Jack came out of the closet. "What did you say?"

"I said there are signs of a struggle in here too," she said and pointed to the bed.

"I'll check with Hill to see if they tested for body fluids and if they got anything we can use from it."

Dried body fluids like semen and vaginal fluids are naturally fluorescent and will actually glow. Therefore, the crime scene investigators use a light source illumination to narrow down the specific locations of stains for collection.

"Now is when we need those cameras. I would *love* to know who Colton made that mess with,"

Diane said as they left the room and went into the office.

"I'd like to know if it was Gayle Eager."

"So would I." Diane followed Jack into the office. "Especially since the security guard said that Colton didn't have any visitors that night."

The first time they were in the office, some items were on Colton's desk. His desktop computer, the phone, pictures, and the lamp were all still on the floor, but the papers were gone. They had been collected and cataloged by the crime scene technicians.

"We need to go through those papers in the morning," Diane said and walked out on the balcony.

"If it was a woman, she must have been pretty strong to push him through that glass and over the balcony," Jack said as he joined her.

"I don't know. I know some strong women." Diane turned and looked inside at the turned-over bookcase and the books that covered the floor. "But I see your point."

"You seen enough?"

"For now," she said, taking off her gloves and leaving the office.

They passed through the living room on the way to the door. Diane glanced at the coffee table where they had seen the circles from the glasses. The fact that there was no forced entry coupled with signs of the struggle in the bedroom told her that not only did Colton know his killer, but also there was a woman involved in some way, and to her thinking, that screamed Gayle and Albert Eager.

The following morning, Diane called the security company. They told her that they would make Jonathan Nolan, the security guard on duty that night, available to be interviewed in their office at eleven that morning. When the detectives arrived, someone escorted them to a conference room where Nolan was waiting. It was a short but illuminating conversation. As Jack expected, Nolan admitted that he left his post twice that evening.

"The first time was right after the cameras went out, and I went in the server room. Sometimes, if you tap it a few times, the cameras come back on, but it didn't work. So I called it in."

"How long would you say that you were away from the desk?" Diane asked.

"Not more than five minutes at most."

"About what time would you say that was?"

"Six fifty-eight."

"You sure of the time?" Jack asked and noted the time.

"I had to call it in and make an entry in the log. So, yeah, I'm sure of the time."

"When was the second time?"

Nolan looked at Jack and Diane and then at the activity going on outside of the conference room. Then he leaned forward.

"I work from four to midnight, and since I'm not supposed to leave the desk, Ian—Ian Cooper, that's my supervisor—is supposed to come around twice a night to relieve me."

"What time is that supposed to happen?"

"Between seven and eight, but last night, it was almost nine, and Ian's a no-show," Nolan said angrily.

"Somehow, I get the feeling that last night wasn't the first time Ian was a no-show," Jack said.

"He does that shit all the time. Most times, he's just late with some unbelievable story, and other times, he just doesn't show at all and has no excuse."

"Why don't you report him?" Diane asked.

"Yeah, right. I still gotta work for him. The last guy that reported Ian for not showing up got transferred to a walking post in Staten Island."

"What time did you leave the desk, and for how long?"

"It was a little after nine, and I was back at nine twenty," Nolan said, and then he went over the basic operating procedures for the detectives.

"So, we know that the killer had at least two opportunities to get in and out of the building that night without being seen," Diane said as she and Jack left the security office.

"And the killer had more than enough time to have a drink, fight, and get out of there."

"Since we know the time the murder was committed, we need to check with CCT and the surrounding businesses to see if any cameras caught the killer coming out of the building," Diane commented on their way to speak with Cecilia Colton and her daughter, Megan.

When the door opened, the detectives were greeted by the Coltons' housekeeper. She escorted them to the study. After offering them their beverage choice, which they refused, she told them to make themselves comfortable, and Mrs. Colton and her daughter would join them shortly.

A few minutes later, Cecilia Colton and her daughter, Megan, came into the room. As Jack and Diane stood up, he extended his hand.

"Mrs. Colton, I'm Detective Harmon, and this is my partner, Detective Mitchell. Let me start by saying that I am sorry for your loss, ma'am."

"Thank you, Detective. And it's Cissy, please," she said and turned to Megan. "And this is my daughter, Megan."

She nodded. "Detectives."

"Please have a seat," Cissy said.

"Thank you," Jack replied as they sat down in the huge, extravagantly decorated living room. Cissy sat down on the couch across from the detectives. Megan sat close to her mother.

"I am very sorry for your loss," Diane said compassionately.

"Thank you, Detective Mitchell," Megan said and squeezed her mother's hand. "As you can imagine, this has all come as quite a shock for our family."

"I understand that this is a very difficult time, so I promise we'll make this as brief as possible," Jack said. *And if you had anything to do with it, we'll be back.*

"It's all right, Detective. I know that you're just doing your job," Cissy said. She took a deep breath and exhaled. "Take as much time as you need and ask whatever you like."

"Thank you, ma'am."

"Cissy, please."

Jack nodded respectfully. "Cissy, is there anything that you can think of that may lead us to your husband's killer? Anybody you can think of that may have had a problem with him over business?" Jack said.

"No, I'm sorry, but nobody comes to mind. Had there been a problem over business, I would have known about it. Elias and I started this company together, and that's how we've run it ever since," she said, dabbing her eyes and thinking that her husband had kept things from her before.

"The last time you spoke to him, how did he seem?"

"He seemed fine to me," she said and glanced at Megan, who nodded her head.

"So, nothing out of the ordinary?" Diane asked and glanced at Jack.

"Tell me about your husband, Mrs. Colton . . . I'm sorry." Jack nodded. "Cissy. Tell me what kind of man he was, his friends, his habits." They were treated to another wonderful testimonial to what a great man Elias Colton was. Wonderful husband and father, prominent businessman and entrepreneur with a long and distinguished track record in his community.

"My father's focus was on encouraging other minority entrepreneurs toward achieving success in business ventures. Titanium is a member of the Association of Black Businesses and has partnerships with minority business development councils nationwide, helping small companies to develop business partnerships to grow their businesses," Megan said like she was reading it straight from the website.

"Damn it, Jack," Diane said as they drove away from the Colton residence. "Instead of wasting all that time listening to that bullshit about what an amazing man Mr. Multiple Indiscretions was, you don't know how badly I wanted to say, let's stop all this bullshit and tell me about Mrs. Gayle Eager."

Jack laughed. "That would have been cruel."

"Bullshit. You saw the wicked scowl on Cissy's face." Diane laughed. "Like she was ready to tell Meggie to shut up and tell us all about her cheating husband."

"You think she knew?"

"Call it a hunch, but, yes, I think Cissy knew *exactly* what her husband was capable of."

"Next, you're going to tell me that a woman just knows these things."

"We do."

"So what now?"

"We go talk to Mrs. Eager," Diane said, and Jack laughed.

"Wouldn't it be great if we just show our badges, and Gayle confesses to everything?"

"That *would* be great. But I was thinking the husband, Albert, is gonna be the one confessing."

"You have a theory?"

"I do."

"Share with me."

"It's a wild one."

"They usually are, but they have a funny way of turning out to be exactly what happened, so share."

"Gayle gets there around seven. They do what cheaters do."

"The bed was tossed."

"Husband gets there after nine. Catches the lovers having an after-sex drink, they fight, and over the balcony Colton goes," Diane said, and Jack chuckled.

"That's actually not that farfetched."

"It's really not farfetched at all."

"Let's go get them. They confess, and we close this one quick," Jack said and settled into the passenger seat.

Chapter Seven

Located in a tranquil waterfront community in New Rochelle with its 6,200 square feet of living space, the seven-bedroom, seven-bath house that had three fireplaces, a sauna, two large outdoor terraces, and a pool that overlooked the Long Island Sound was the new home of Michael and Cassandra, a.k.a. Shy, Black and their family.

While Shy was under investigation for the murder of Andrade Ferreira, explosives were planted on each side of their old house. Shortly after Black and Shy got home, the first bomb detonated. It took out almost half of the house. The boys' room, as well as M's room, were gone due to the explosion. It was only due to the second detonator malfunction that Black and Shy were able to escape.

When they came out of their bedroom, they could see that the rest of the house, including the staircase, was on fire. Thinking quickly, Shy led them into Michelle's room and went out on the balcony, where they could climb down on the vine-covered lattice. Once the bombers realized that the second bomb didn't explode, they reestablished the connection and pressed the detonator button. The second bomb exploded. The explosion shook them off their feet, but they survived.

"Somebody has to pay for this, Michael," Shy told her husband that night as Chuck drove them away from their burning house, and she was as good as her word when those responsible felt her wrath.

Now that they had bought a home and were back living in the city, Mr. and Mrs. Black had gotten back to quietly running their legitimate businesses. In addition to that, Black had taken more of an active interest in The Family. Once Shy decided to hang up her guns, it was easy for him to turn his back and walk away because, after all, being with Shy and raising their children was all that he'd wanted since the first time he laid eyes on her.

That evening, Mr. and Mrs. Black were getting ready to go to an Association of Black Businesses event to celebrate the inauguration of their new president, Elaine Cargill. As Black began becoming more involved in the legitimate part of his business, Congressman, now Senator-elect Martin Marshall, urged Black to join the association to further their business interests. In the short time since Meka took him to his first meeting, Black had become quite influential, working behind the scenes, forming alliances that would benefit him and the long-term goal that he'd set for his legitimate business interests.

Elaine Cargill was also one of the founding, most active, and most influential members of the Association of Black Businesses. She was the president and chairperson of the board of Absolutely Essential Beauty Products, a company that she started that used to make fake jewelry and now manufactured and distributed a line of hair and skin-care products for women of color worldwide. Many felt it was just her time, but the truth behind her ascension to the presidency was that she was Martin Marshall's choice to lead the association. Unfortunately, he had a problem working with Joseph Connor, the association's previous president. Therefore, when it came time for elections, Elaine was encouraged to run. With the help of Mike Black, who whipped votes for her, Elaine easily won on the first ballot.

Shy sat in front of her vanity mirror, putting on the finishing touches of her makeup. That evening, the lovely Mrs. Black had selected a long sleeve, purple Raisa Vanessa mock neck gown with embellished velvet zigzag accents and a thigh-high slit. She never liked attending events like this. *I just don't like being around a bunch of women trying to get in my business.* But now that their son Mansa was a year old, Shy had run out of excuses.

She went with Mike the first time to keep her promise and be supportive because she saw how important the association had become to him. However, once she had attended a few events, Shy had made connections with other businessmen and women, and from that, she saw opportunities to expand her import-export business. Therefore, Shy had become more comfortable attending.

"As long as you don't leave my side for very long, and when you have to, you promise to come right back."

Dressed in a Fendi two-piece tuxedo, Mr. Black sat in the living room with a lot on his mind waiting for his stunning wife to come down the stairs. First and foremost on his mind was that Michelle was out with friends in the new car they got her for her sixteenth birthday. It wasn't that he worried about her as a driver. Michelle had been driving cars in the Bahamas since she could see over the dashboard and reach the pedal at the same time. Instead, it was where her newfound freedom would take his little girl that worried him.

This is just something that you're gonna have to get used to, he thought and hoped that he and Shy had taught their daughter to make good choices. But Michelle, like her cousin Barbara, had become curious about the world that her father was boss of. And *that* was what worried him.

Although he was still recognized as the boss of The Family, he had given the power and the title that came with it to Rain Robinson. She was the boss of The Family now, and he functioned as her consigliere. Black had sat out the war with Rona King until she made the mistake of targeting Shy while she was pregnant with Mansa and shooting Jada West. A few days later, Barnes and Mobley were dead, and Hawkins was on the run. When the police arrested Rain for the murder of Afra Dean, it was Black that brokered the deal with Rona King that ended the war. And he had given Rain a free hand to deal with the repercussions of Twan, a top lieutenant in the Caldwell Enterprise getting murdered at Conversations.

However, since returning from the extended vacation he and Shy took with Bobby and Pam in the South Pacific, Black stayed on top of what was going on with Kojo. The natural assumption around The Family was that it involved Angelo and The Curcio Family, but it was so much deeper than that.

And then you can tell me what I already know was the question that Black asked Jackie when he learned that Rain had involved The Family in the assassinations of Caldwell associates, Drum and Greg Mac.

For years, I've been telling her that she needs a better disguise than a blond wig and big glasses.

Although Jackie apologized for her disloyalty in not telling him, Black told her that it wasn't a story for her to tell. Black thought that it was something that he should have heard from Rain a long time ago. It made him question more than just her judgment.

And *that* worried him too.

"I'm ready," Shy said as she came down the steps, and with that, Chuck got up and headed for the door.

Black stood up. "You look amazing, my love," he said as he walked toward the steps and took her hand.

"Thank you, Michael," she said. He escorted her to the Mercedes-Maybach GLS 600 SUV for the trip to the Greenwich Ballroom of The Four Seasons Hotel to attend Elaine's inauguration.

Upon arrival at the ballroom, Black and Shy entered the lift that took them from street level directly to the elegant Grand Ballroom, with its wall-to-wall windows. As he approached their table, Black was surprised but not shocked to see Marvin's lawyer, Ebony Maddox, sitting next to Quentin Hunter. Meka had introduced him that first night he attended an association meeting. They were both in the real estate business, and the two formed a friendship. Quentin had heard of Black and was impressed that Black was a businessman and not the thug he expected. In the time since, their mutual interest in business, money, and politics had only proved to strengthen their bond.

Quentin met Ebony Maddox at Michelle's birthday party, and Black had noticed that Quentin was taken with her immediately. So taken that he invited her to attend the event tonight as his guest. To say that Quentin was surprised that she came really didn't truly capture the magnitude of what he felt when she was escorted to the table. Although he was twenty years her senior, Ebony thought he was a very handsome and intelligent man whose company she'd enjoyed that evening. And she had to agree with Quentin when he said that being a member of the Association of Black Businesses would be good for her fledgling law firm.

And besides, the whole salt-and-pepper goatee thing against that deep chocolate skin is sexy as hell, Ebony thought the night they met, so there she was.

Quentin stood up and shook Black's hand. "How are you, Mike?"

"Doing great. What about you?"

"I'm doing fine today. And Cassandra," he said, taking her hand and bowing slightly, "always a pleasure to see you."

"How are you, Quentin?" she replied as Black pulled out the chair, and she sat down.

"I'm doing very well tonight," he said and glanced at Ebony.

"How are you doing tonight, Ebony?" Black asked and sat down next to her.

"I'm doing fine, Mike." Ebony leaned forward. "How are you, Mrs. Black?"

"I'm doing wonderful tonight, Ebony," she said. "And please, call me Shy."

Ebony smiled. "I certainly will."

"I love that dress on you," Shy said of the royal blue Chiara Boni Gosia one-shoulder gown Ebony was wearing.

"Thank you, Mrs. . . . I mean Shy. You look amazing too."

"Thank you, Ebony," Shy said as another member arrived and was seated at their table.

"Hi, everybody," Andrea Frazier said as she sat down next to Quentin.

"How are you, Andrea?" Black and Shy said almost at the same time.

"I'm awesome," she replied as she always did.

"Ebony Maddox," Quentin began, "I'd like you to meet Andrea Frazier."

Ebony reached across Quentin to shake her hand. "Nice to meet you, Andrea."

"Nice to meet you too, Ebony."

"Andrea is the chief operating officer at Rockville Guaranty Savings and Loan," Quentin informed her.

"An *overworked* chief operating officer," Andrea replied with a smile.

"And just where is that slave-driver boss of yours?" he asked, referring to Daniel Beason, chairman of the board at Rockville.

"I haven't spoken with him today, but I'm sure he and Susan will be here soon."

"Speaking of which, where is Elias?" Quentin inquired.

"I'm sure he'll be along too. You know as well as I do that Elias never misses any of the association's functions." Andrea leaned close to Quentin. "With Cissy being out in Colorado, there's no telling what trouble he's gotten into."

"Ain't that the truth," Quentin whispered.

"Especially not tonight," Black added.

"You're right. He worked hard to see this day come for Elaine," Quentin commented as the house lights dimmed a little.

After some brief announcements, Elaine Cargill was inaugurated as the new president of the Association of Black Businesses. During her acceptance speech, she announced that this year's association fundraiser would support a yet-to-be-named community center that was currently under construction.

Ebony smiled as she listened to Elaine define the projects. She knew from the description of the center that it was the project that Marvin's construction company, Pearson MDS Construction, was working on. She looked at Black, who was smiling proudly, and Ebony correctly assumed that he not only had something to do with Pearson MDS being awarded the contract, but he was also directly involved in the association funding it as well.

After her concluding remarks, the new president received a standing ovation, and shortly after that, dinner was served. When the staff began serving, Daniel Beason and his wife, Susan, arrived at the table.

"Sorry we're late," Beason said and sat down next to Andrea. "We almost didn't come."

"It was such a crazy day," Susan said and smiled as she waved across the table at Mr. and Mrs. Black. Shy had noticed how Susan looked at her husband and that he barely acknowledged her presence. Although she thought it was sad, Mrs. Beason was somebody that needed to be watched.

"But I thought it would be good for Danny to get out instead of sitting around the house on a day like this."

"What was so crazy about it?" Andrea asked.

"We found out that Elias Colton was murdered," Beason said.

"*What?*" Andrea exclaimed.

Black and Shy looked at each other and then back at Beason.

"How?" Quentin asked.

"I don't know anything about the details, but Doris said someone pushed him from the balcony of his midtown condo," Beason said and looked at Andrea. "It was a very hard day."

"I'm sorry for your loss. I know you and Elias were close," Shy said to Beason, but she still hadn't taken her eyes off Susan, and she hadn't taken hers off Black.

Chapter Eight

Jack and Diane were sitting in their car parked just down the street from Saint Luke's Episcopal Church, where the funeral service for Elias Colton was held. They arrived there early so they could get a good place to watch as people entered the church. Colton was a popular man, so many people were milling about and entering the church. Both detectives thought that who showed up for your funeral not only said a lot about the person but also would often lead them to their killer. They were hoping that this would be the case that day.

They had tried to interview Albert and Gayle Eager, but it didn't happen because neither was available. Diane had spoken to Albert, and he was willing to meet with her, but he was in Connecticut supervising a new contract they'd been awarded. As for Gayle, she never answered her phone, nor did she return any of Jack's calls.

"I'll be interested to see if she shows," Jack said.

"And if she does, will Albert be with her?"

"They were all friends." Jack chuckled. "At least they were *before* Colton started fucking his wife."

"I hear some men take that type of thing very seriously. Which I don't understand since some of those same men want to stick their dick in every woman they see," Diane commented.

"No man wants another man in his pussy," Jack laughed. "Especially when he finds one that fits," he said and patted Diane's mound.

"May I remind you, sir, that we are outside of a church," Diane said and giggled. Then she took a picture of Quentin Hunter going inside the church. He had been with his children at the time of the murder, so he was easily eliminated as a suspect.

"We are parked down the street approximately three hundred yards from a church watching funeral goers through binoculars and taking pictures with a 50-mm lens."

"What's your point?" Diane said as she snapped a picture of Joseph Connor and his wife, Georgia, as they entered the church. Like just about everybody they'd spoken with, Georgia had nothing but great things to say about Elias Colton. However, that wasn't the case when it came to Joseph. As the former president of the Association of Black Businesses, Connor had dealt with Colton for years and hated his guts. That may or may not have something to do with the fact that Elias had fucked Georgia too. That would have made him a suspect, but he had an alibi for the time of the murder.

"My point is that I don't think this qualifies as outside of a church," he said using air quotes.

Diane took a picture of Elaine Cargill and her husband, Walter, going inside the church. They had spoken with her the day before, and she gladly treated them to another glowing Elias Colton tribute. However, Elaine's entire demeanor changed when Jack asked for access to a list of their membership.

"Do you have a warrant, Detective Harmon?" was her answer.

Jack picked up his binoculars as a Mercedes-Maybach parked outside the church, and a man got out.

"I like that model Benz," he said as the man opened the door, and a woman stepped out. But it was when another man came around the SUV that his eyes opened wide. "Whoa."

"What?"

"What is *he* doing here?"

"Who?" Diane said and raised her camera. "Oh shit," she said as Mike and Cassandra Black walked hand in hand into Saint Luke's.

"This changes things considerably."

"In a *big* way," Diane said as she took several pictures of Black and Shy going into the church. "You think he's involved?"

"Him personally, are you kidding? Black doesn't get his hands dirty anymore. He doesn't have to.

There are plenty of people that are more than willing to live and die at his command," Jack said, and Diane wondered what inspires that kind of loyalty.

"You're right. He'd send somebody." Diane thought about her crime scene and shook her head. "Too messy. This was over something personal. I can feel it."

"But just the fact that he's here means that we have to consider the possibility that The Family—"

"Or members of it—"

"Might be involved," Jack added.

"I think it's necessary that we eliminate him and The Family as suspects," Diane said and thought about the fact that despite being a well-known criminal, the two people that she was closest to, her partner Jack, and Carmen Taylor, had enormous respect for Mike Black, and she needed to understand why.

"But we shouldn't jump to any conclusions."

"Agreed," Diane said. "We still investigate this case like any other. That just means we investigate with the knowledge that they might be involved in some way."

"Agreed," Jack said as Gayle Eager and her husband, Albert, arrived at the church.

The Eagers had known Elias Colton and his wife Cissy for years. They were a part of the partnership between Titanium Distributing Service and smaller companies that Colton personally selected to develop and grow their businesses. The Eagers were the owner-operators of an industrial and housecleaning janitorial service and were excited to be chosen to participate in the program.

Soon, Elias was mentoring Albert and Gayle in the ways of the business world and was largely, if not solely, responsible for the expansion of their business into the tristate area. As he had for so many others in the program, Elias made them rich because connections and relationships are everything in business. With their industrial service business expanding into New Jersey and Connecticut, Albert's focus turned to managing the growth, and Colton's focus turned to Gayle, and the affair began.

"There they are," Diane said and took a couple of shots of them walking toward the church. "And they're together. Holding hands and looking all chummy."

"Can you zoom in on her face?" Jack asked. "I wanna see her expression," he said, and Diane caught the image.

"She looks more disgusted than she does sad to me," Diane commented and showed the image to Jack.

"I see what you mean. What do you think it says about her and her mood?"

"If I had to guess . . . and this is based on them being my primary suspects, I think that she's disgustcd that shc has to be here holding hands and making nice with the man that killed her lover."

"You got all that from looking at that picture?"

"I did," she said and captured an image of Andrea Frazier arriving and going inside, followed by Daniel Beason and his wife, Susan. "Who are they?"

"Based on the description we got from Cissy and Doris Bessemer, that would be Daniel and Susan Beason," Jack said, watching Susan's thick thighs in the yellow Alexandre Vauthier ruched velvet minidress and matching Gianvito Rossi ribbon acrylic and metallic leather slingback pumps.

"I see what you mean. Arrogant to the point of being an asshole and overdressed to the point of being over the top." Diane zoomed in on them and captured another image. "She could have at least worn black. Yellow screams 'look at me.'"

Just out of curiosity, Diane went inside Saint Luke's and heard Father Went read from Ecclesiastes, chapter twelve.

"The silver cord of life is broken, the golden bowl is crushed, the pitcher at the fountain is shattered, and the wheel at the cistern is crushed. Then the dust out of which God made man's body will return to the earth as it was, and the spirit will return to God who gave it."

As the service concluded and the funeral goers began filing out of the church, Jack and Diane had a decision to make.

"How you wanna play this?" Diane asked and saw Gayle and Albert coming out of the church. She noticed that they weren't holding hands anymore. In fact, she was walking just a little ahead of him, and she was crying.

Jack put down his binoculars and turned to Diane. "As bad as I want to, I don't think we should approach Gayle and Albert here."

"Crying the way she is, I don't think that we'll get much out of her anyway," Diane said and snapped off a couple of shots of them until they were out of sight.

"I think that we should talk to them separately."

"Which one do you want?" Diane asked, expecting him to want to talk to Gayle, and she'd take Albert because that's the way they usually did it.

"I'll take Albert. You got a good insight into her frame of mind." Jack paused.

"My insight is that she knows Albert did it."

"So, what do you want to do now?"

"I want to talk to him," Diane said and pointed as Black and Shy came out of the church. "Come on before he gets away," she said, and the detectives exited their vehicle and walked quickly toward the church.

They picked up their pace when they saw Chuck pull up in the Maybach. As they made their way to the SUV, Black and Shy stopped to talk to Quentin Hunter.

"Excuse me, Mr. Black," Diane said politely.

Black recognized her voice immediately. "Detective Mitchell." He turned and smiled. "How are you?"

"I'm fine, Mr. Black."

"Cassandra, this is Detective Mitchell."

"It's a pleasure to meet you, Mrs. Black."

Shy smiled politely and nodded in acknowledgment but seeing that she never liked cops, she said nothing to Diane. Besides, she was Carmen Taylor's friend, and Carmen Taylor wasn't one of her favorite people. *To know that my husband used to date the world's most beautiful woman is a bit intimidating.* Shy told Black that the night she met Carmen was the first time in her life that she felt inadequate.

I'm glad she's married. Now, all I have to worry about is Jada West.

"And Jack. You remember Jack?"

"Jack."

"Hello, Shy."

"How are you, Jack?" Black asked and shook his hand. Then he turned to Quentin. "Would you excuse us? I need to speak with the detectives."

Quentin chuckled. "No problem, Mike." They shook hands. "I'll get with you in a day or two."

"Sounds good."

"Cassandra, a pleasure as always," Quentin said.

"Just sorry it has to be under these circumstances. Michael tells me that you and Elias were close. You have my deepest condolences," Shy said and glanced at Chuck. He opened the back door, and she got in.

"Good to see you again, Mr. Hunter," Diane said. Quentin nodded. "Detectives."

"Now," Black said as Quentin walked away, "what can I do for you, Detectives?"

"Just curious to know what your association was with Elias Colton," Diane said, and Black laughed.

"Instead of me faking like I'm indignant because you haven't asked anybody else what their association was with him, Detective Mitchell, I'll just tell you that I met Elias a few years ago at a meeting of the Association of Black Businesses. An organization that I'm a member of."

"Really?" Diane smiled. "You're a member?"

"And that surprises you?" Black asked and folded his arms across his chest.

"No, Mr. Black. Nothing that you do surprises me," Diane said, but it did make her wonder if he was the reason Elaine Cargill refused to disclose her membership without a warrant.

"But to answer your question, I'm here because Elias was my friend, and I came here to celebrate his life. You know, like all the rest of the people that you *didn't* ask."

"Apologies. I'm sorry for your loss. Everybody, and I do mean everybody, tells me what a great man he was."

"I take people as they come, Detective Mitchell."

"Would you be willing to talk to me about his murder?" Diane smiled. "Because, honestly, and I mean you no disrespect, between the three of us, you know more about murder than either of us. I'd be very interested in hearing your insights."

Black laughed. "I see why Carmen likes you."

"I understand why she likes you," Diane said, but she didn't laugh. *She used to love him.*

Black took a business card from his jacket pocket and handed it to the detective. "Erykah Morgan?" Diane questioned. "That an alias or something?"

"She's my executive assistant. Just give her a call anytime, and she'll take care of you. I am at your disposal anytime." He turned to Jack with his hand out. "Good to see you again, Jack."

"Good to see you too, Mike," he said as Chuck opened the door, and Black got in.

Chapter Nine

"You know they think you did it," Shy said as Chuck drove away from Saint Luke's.

"Me? They probably think *you* did it. You know, with *your* history of violence, you're probably their number one suspect."

"You're probably right. Can't find your killer . . . go arrest Shy."

"Exactly my point."

"But I know you don't want to talk about a history of violence. Not you."

"I don't know what you're talking about," Black said with a straight face.

"*Really*, Michael?"

"Really. I'm a law-abiding citizen. *You're* the one with the history of violence."

"History of violence." Shy shook her head. "Which one of us used to be called 'Vicious Black'?"

"That was a long time ago, Cassandra. Long before I met you."

"I know. Long before you met me, you had a history of violence."

"You're the one that just got out of jail for murder—"

"That I didn't commit," she said quickly.

"And what was the first thing you did when you got out? You ran down to Rio and killed somebody."

"I got out of jail after you stabbed somebody to death with a glass."

Black laughed. "Damn sure did."

"See, history of violence. You, Mike Black. *Not* Cassandra Black, Mike, they used to call me Vicious Black."

"You were in jail because of him."

"And he blew up our house."

"I really don't think they should count. What do you think, Chuck?"

"I think it's best if I stay out of this," he said and kept driving.

"Smart. And you'd be smart to let this go before we start comparing body counts."

"I think Father Went gave Elias a nice send-off."

"Smart. I always knew you were smart."

"Isn't that why you married me?"

"I married you for those foot massages." Shy took both of his hands in hers. "Your hands are magic."

"So you told me."

"So what did the cops want?"

"They want to talk to me about Elias's murder."

Shy laughed. "They think you did it?"

"I know Elias and I are criminals."

"And you're a killer at that."

"If I were a cop, I'd want to talk to me too," Black said as Chuck got on I-95 for the twenty-minute ride to New Rochelle.

When they got to the house, the first thing that Black noticed was that Michelle's car was not parked in the driveway. He glanced over at Shy and could tell by the frown on her face that she saw it too. She was against getting her the car.

She's only 16, Michael. What does she need with a car?

Neither Black nor Shy said anything about it, but she gave him her *I'm mad at you, Michael* look and simply got out of the car when Chuck opened her door. Since he had gotten the look, Black took his time getting out of the Maybach and walked a little behind Shy as they went inside. Although he had taken steps to make sure Michelle was safe, he worried about her every time she left the house. But by this time, he agreed with his wife that their 16-year-old daughter really didn't need a car. But there was no way in hell he was going to give her the satisfaction of telling her that.

The house was quiet when they walked in. "We're home," Shy said loudly and got no answer. Then she heard a noise coming from the kitchen.

As Black went upstairs to change, Shy went to the kitchen. When she got there, M was in her usual spot cooking. She loved to cook, and that day, she was making Chicken Spinach Artichoke Lasagna for the family's dinner.

"Hey, M," Shy said and got a bottle of water from the refrigerator.

"Cassandra," a startled M said and turned toward her daughter-in-law, "I didn't hear you come in."

"I called when we got home, but I guess you didn't hear me."

"I guess not," M said, thinking that she didn't hear as well as she used to and thought about getting her hearing checked the next time she visited her doctor.

"Where is everybody?"

"Joanne and Mansa are taking a nap, and Easy is in his room doing whatever it is that he does in there."

"Where's Michelle?"

"She ran out of here about an hour ago. She said that she was going to study with Tiera."

"Right," Shy said and left the kitchen rolling her eyes and M smiling because Joanne had told her how Shy used to stay in the streets when she was Michelle's age and how it used to drive her crazy.

Michelle was a junior at the Onyx Academy of Higher Learning, which was in her father's old neighborhood. It was a community-based school that Reverend Darrell Jones founded because he felt that the education that students were getting in traditional schools was not adequately preparing most of them for work and life. The school offered students a state-approved curriculum and taught from an Afro-centric point of view. After he and Shy enrolled Michelle and Easy, Black's company, Prestige Capital and Associates, donated property for a new school. Then Prestige built the new location to the reverend's specifications and funded their payroll, both of which were tax-deductible. Those donations freed the school to use other contributions and grants for students' tuition, books, computers, and other equipment.

Michelle had been a student there off and on since she was 5 and getting ready to start preschool. She was a good student, mostly As and Bs, with the occasional C—which was unacceptable to her parents. Although she spent more of her school years in the Bahamas, she was well liked by her teachers and was one of the more popular girls at school. But that wasn't always the case. When she was in middle school and returned to Onyx after going to school in the Bahamas for a couple of years, Michelle had to reestablish herself with some of the new girls. She had been back at school for a week, and people noticed that Michelle and Easy were driven to school by Chuck, who got out of the car and opened the door for them.

"Who you think you are, rich girl?" one girl asked.

"I'm sure I'm Michelle Black," she said and turned to walk away.

When she did, the girl punched her in the back of her head. Michelle was startled by the blow and stumbled forward. She turned to see the girl laughing with her hands up, ready to fight. But before Michelle could do anything about it, a teacher intervened, separated the girls, and took them to the office. She had witnessed the entire exchange, and the other girl was given detention.

When Chuck picked up Michelle that afternoon and saw her hair and clothes in a mess, he asked her what had happened, and she told him that she had a fight. After Chuck asked how long detention was, he took her and Easy to get a slice of their favorite pizza, pepperoni with extra cheese. Once they finished eating, they were back in the car, but instead of taking them home, he took her back to the school.

"What are we doing back here?" Michelle asked when he parked.

"You weren't planning on letting her get away with sneaking you like that, were you?" Chuck said, looking at his watch. "Detention is over."

Michelle smiled and got out of the car, and when the girl came out of the building with the other detention goers, she was waiting. When she got back to the car, Michelle's hair and clothes were a mess. She may have had a couple of scratches on her face, but Michelle established that she was *not* the one. Michelle was no longer the rich girl with the driver. She was the girl that *nobody* wanted to mess with, but *everybody* wanted to hang out with. Later that evening, when Black and Shy got home and saw her face, Black had two questions.

"What happened to you?"

"I had a fight."

"Did you win?"

"Yes."

"Good," Black said, and that was it for him. Shy, on the other hand, had further questions.

"Not so fast, young lady," she said as Michelle started to walk away. "Had a fight with who, over what?" Shy demanded to know and made her explain, in detail, exactly what happened. Michelle told her story, and Shy commented that she was going to have words with Chuck.

"And then I beat her ass," was how Michelle ended the story.

"Don't curse in front of your mother," Black said.

"Yes, Daddy."

Shy looked at Black. "So I guess your daughter out fighting in the street is all right with you?"

"She won, didn't she?" Black asked, and Michelle smiled.

Shy looked at her daughter and her husband. "You and your daughter need to get out of my sight."

"Yes, Mommy," Michelle said, and Black stood up. They left Shy alone in the living room, thinking about her days in school and the trouble she used to get into those days.

About seven o'clock later that evening, Black and Shy were in the media room watching a movie when they heard the front door open and close.

"That you, Michelle?" Shy yelled.

"Yes, Mommy," Michelle yelled back as she ran up the stairs.

Five minutes later, she came charging down the stairs and headed for the door.

"I'll be back," Michelle yelled, and Shy bounced out of her chair and rushed out of the room.

Black shook his head. Joanne had told him her stories about teenage Shy too.

She caught Michelle before she could make it out the door. "Where do you think you're going?"

"Back to Tiera's house to finish studying," Michelle said and held up *Barron's Regents Exams And Answers* book. "I forgot this book, and I need it to study."

"Doesn't Tiera have one?"

"She left it at school, and Sharkiesha lost hers. We tried to find a version online that we could study from, but we couldn't find any," Michelle said and watched her mother's eyes narrow. *She's not going for it,* she thought, but then Shy exhaled.

"I'm not gonna have you running in and out of this house, you hear me?"

"Yes, Mommy."

"The least you could do is show your father and me enough respect to come and say hello to us and let us know what you're doing. Maybe even ask if it's all right with us that you drive back to Tiera's house to study at this time of night. You might think you're grown, but you're not."

"Yes, Mommy," Michelle said respectfully, thinking that Shy was about to flip and say she couldn't go out again.

"Don't just stand there and 'yes, Mommy' me and then turn around and do what you want," Shy said to Michelle and realized that Joanne had said those exact words to her.

I hate it when her words come rolling out of my mouth.

"Yes, Mommy—I mean, no, Mommy, I won't. Next time, I will come and let you and Daddy know where I'm going and what I'm doing."

"What time are you coming home?"

"I'll be home by ten," Michelle said, knowing that it would be more like eleven or twelve before she got home. She held her breath.

"Make sure you're back by ten, young lady." Michelle exhaled and tried not to smile. "I don't want to have this conversation with you again, you understand me?" Joanne had said that too.

"Yes, Mommy," Michelle said and hugged Shy. "Love you, Mommy," she said, then left the house as Shy went back to the media room. Michelle ran to her car and got in.

"How'd it go?" Sharkiesha asked as Michelle started the car.

"We're good. I thought for a minute that I wasn't gonna make it back out. But I think the geometry book was what sold it." Michelle drove off.

"What were we gonna do if she didn't let you back out?" Sharkiesha asked.

"One of Daddy's men would take you home."

"That wouldn't have been cool," Sharkiesha said.

"Did you get the clothes?" Michelle asked.

"I got them," Tiera said and held up the bag of clothes that Michelle had dropped off her balcony.

They weren't going back to Tiera's house to finish studying geometry. They were done with that for the day. When the idea of going to the movies came up, Michelle said she had to change her clothes.

Back inside the house, Black looked up as Shy returned to the media room and started the movie they were watching. Then he saw the frustration in her eyes, and knowing what was going to happen next, he paused the movie. She stopped in front of Black and pointed at him.

"This is *your* fault."

"Me? What did *I* do?"

"I told you that she didn't need a car." Shy went and sat down in the chair next to him. "But, no, you had to go and buy *your baby girl* that damn car. Now, you can't keep her out of the streets. She's gone all the time."

"Hmm."

Shy gave him the look. "What's *that* supposed to mean, Michael?"

"It means, hmm."

"I know what you're thinking. Go ahead and say it. You agree with my mother, don't you? You think I got this coming, don't you? 'Now you got a child that acts exactly like you used to act,'" Shy said sarcastically, repeating what Joanne had been saying to her for years, and she was tired of hearing it.

"I wasn't going to say that. I was just going to ask where she said she was going."

"She *said* she was going back to Tiera's house to finish studying geometry, but I know better." Shy laughed. "Even had a geometry book with her. She just don't realize that I know all her little tricks and a bunch she hasn't even thought of. Standing there trying to look innocent. 'Yes, Mommy, yes, Mommy,' knowing she's gonna run outta here and do the opposite of what I told her to do."

"Not that I'm agreeing with her, but you know you're proving Joanne's point, right?"

"Shut up, Michael, and start the movie." When Black started the movie, Shy said, "I know she's right. Dale, Chee-Chee, and I used to stay in the streets, and it used to drive Mommy crazy. That doesn't mean that I have to like it." Shy punched him in the arm. "At least I didn't have a car to run the streets in. We had to take the damn train."

Black pointed at her. "History of violence."

"Shut up, Michael, and start the movie."

"Just saying," he said and rewound the movie to the point before Michelle came in the house.

And then there was peace.

Chapter Ten

Even though she made Carter believe that she was rushing off to talk to Millie that night at J.R.'s after she told him that she was pregnant, it was actually a couple of days later when Ricky parked the car in front of Millie Claxton's house. Alwan got out to open the car door for her. The truth was she was tired of talking to him because there was nothing else to say.

And besides, the smell of him is making me feel sick.

It had been a good morning so far, which recently meant that she hadn't thrown up that day. Rain noticed that her breasts were tender, that she had been tired and irritable, more irritable than usual anyway, but it was when nausea and vomiting began that she realized that she was late, and she went to see Daniella Ramsey.

"And nobody needs to know about this. Not even Perry, you understand?"

"I understand," Daniella said, nodding her head quickly as if Rain had a gun in her face.

It was true, Rain Robinson scared the shit out of her, so her hands were shaking a bit, and her heart was still racing when Rain left the office.

"Wait here; I won't be long," she said to Alwan, and Rain started for the house.

Alwan was glad that part of her effort to avoid Carter was to take them with her wherever she went, so he considered the breakup a blessing because it was easier to protect her. She took out her keys as she approached the house, rang the bell once, and then let herself in.

"Millie," Rain shouted as she walked through the house. "Millie."

Millie came out of the kitchen, drying her hands. "Glad it wasn't nothing important," Millie said. "And stop all that damn hollering in my house."

"You didn't make it seem like it was important. You just said stop by, and there was something that you wanted to talk to me about." Rain sat down. "I asked if everything was all right, and you said, 'Yes, Lorraine, everything is fine,' so here I am."

"You want something to drink?"

"No, I'm fine," Rain said. Millie looked at her strangely because she had never turned down a drink. Making herself a drink was usually the first thing Rain did when she came through the door. "What did you want to talk to me about?"

Millie sat down in the chair across from Rain. "Your family."

Rain's eyes got wide. "Something wrong with Lakeda and the kids?" she asked of her sister-in-law and her children.

"Lakeda's fine, and Miles Junior and Rasheeda are just grown and fast."

"You all right?"

"I told you, I'm fine, Lorraine. I'm talking about your *other* family."

Rain sat up straight. "What about them?"

Millie laughed. "Relax, Lorraine, I'm talking about your *mother's* family."

Rain sucked her teeth. "What family? I ain't heard from any of them muthafuckas . . . ever. So why should I give a fuck about any of them?"

"Because they're your blood," Millie said, and Rain laughed.

"My blood is the niggas I done shed blood with and for. *That's* my family."

"I am not about to sit here and tell you that you're wrong—"

"Thank you."

"But just hear me out."

"Okay, go ahead," Rain said, but she really didn't want to hear anything that Millie had to say about her mother's family. The way Rain saw it was they didn't want anything to do with her and her brother Miles, so fuck them.

"Yes, they turned their backs on you and Miles when you were kids, but you have to remember back in those days," Millie chuckled. "I guess you were too young to remember those days."

"I don't even remember my mother, much less those days." Rain paused to think for a second. "Daddy never would say much about her," she laughed. "Other than 'your mama was a no-good whore, and we were better off without her.' He never had anything good to say about her."

"Jasper was a very angry man, especially when it came to your mother."

"What was she like?"

"Your mother was . . ." Millie paused because in all the years that she'd known Rain, and she'd known Rain all her life, she'd never once asked about her mother. "She was beautiful. She was good people, sweet and kindhearted, but Barbara Langston loved to party, and she loved her some men." Millie smiled as she thought back on the days when she was young, and they used to run together. "Your father knew that about Barbara when he met her. But your father was your father, and he had to have her, and he knew that he could bend Barbara to his will like he did every other woman he met." Millie shook her head. "Not Barbara, though. She had too much spirit for Jasper to tame."

"So what happened?"

"Between your father and your mother?"

"Yeah, Millie. You know what I'm asking you. Did my father really kill my mother?"

Millie exhaled. "I don't know, Lorraine. That was the talk back then, but I don't know."

"What happened?"

"When your father met your mother, Barbara was dating a guy named Eddie Mars. But like I said, when Jasper saw her, he had to have her. So Jasper went hard at her, throwing money at her, taking her on trips, buying her whatever she wanted. Clothes, jewelry, a new Mustang convertible," Millie laughed. "We used to call her 'Mustang Barbara.' Anyway, whatever she wanted, he got it for her."

Rain laughed because she'd seen him buy a woman's affection that way. "Like he did Kelly Joyner."

"Exactly." She laughed. "That bitch," Millie said of a woman that J.R. dated that hung around just long enough to make Rain's early teenage years miserable. "Anyway, when Jasper asked her to marry him a couple of months later, she said yes, and they got married." Millie paused and looked at Rain. "But Barbara was still in love with Eddie. Everybody but Jasper could see it. But the heart wants what the heart wants, and she never did stop seeing Eddie, even after she and your father were married."

Rain understood, all too well, what that felt like to want a man that belonged to somebody else. Even though Nick was with Wanda when she met him, Rain had to have him. And once she got him, Rain would tell anybody that Nick was hers, and there wasn't a damn thing Wanda could do about it.

"When Barbara got pregnant with your brother, Miles, and she had the baby, Jasper said he didn't look anything like him. No matter who and how many people told him that the baby just looked more like his mother, your father was convinced that the baby looked like Eddie. He slapped Barbara around at the hospital, and then he left the hospital and went after Eddie yelling, 'I'll kill that muthafucka!'"

"Did he kill him?"

"Not that night. Jasper caught up with him at a bar. They both did a lot of shouting; guns were drawn, a few shots were fired, but, no, he didn't kill him. After that, Eddie stayed away from Barbara and out of Jasper's way. So when Barbara got pregnant again and had you, Jasper was cool because you came out looking just like your daddy. But like I said, the heart wants what the heart wants, and Barbara started seeing Eddie behind his back again. It went on for over a year before your father found out about it."

"How'd he find out?"

Millie looked at Rain and swallowed hard.

"The night she was killed, she, Blue, and I were at . . . some bar," Millie laughed. "I don't even remember the name of it now because it was so long ago. But anyway, Eddie was there, and the two of them were sneaking glances at each other. So when Blue got up and went to get a drink, Eddie rushed up to the table and told your mother to meet him in the usual place, and then he left. When Blue got back, Barbara made up some excuse and rushed out of there to be with Eddie."

"Blue told my father."

"The police found her and Eddie dead in a motel room. They said that it was a murder-suicide. The cops said that Barbara shot him once in the dick and once in the chest, and then she shot herself in the head. But the word on the street was that your father found them at that motel and killed them both."

Rain sat there silently for a while.

"You think it's true?" Rain asked.

"I don't know, Lorraine. All I can tell you is that was the talk back then."

"I know. He killed her," Rain said, knowing all too well how heartless her father could be when he needed or wanted to be.

Once again, there was silence in the room as Rain thought, and Millie didn't know what to say.

So she sat there, looking at Rain and wondering what she was thinking. Millie couldn't even imagine what it felt like to know that your father killed your mother.

"What about my mother's family?" Rain finally asked. Somehow, hearing the story made her feel close to her mother for the first time in her life. Like they had something in common.

"Your mother's sister, your aunt Priscilla, Priscilla Langston—" Millie began.

"Y'all still speak?" Rain interrupted.

"Yes. Not daily or anything like that, but we stay in touch."

"Why am I just hearing about this?"

"Because you didn't give a fuck about them until five minutes ago."

"I still don't give a fuck about them, but what about her?"

"She has a daughter. Her name is Sapphire, and she hasn't heard from her in a couple of weeks. She's worried about her."

"You're right. I don't give a fuck about somebody I don't give a fuck about being missing," Rain said and stood up.

"Sit your black ass down, Lorraine."

"Yes, ma'am," Rain said and sat down again.

"Now, I know you don't give a fuck, and you have no reason to give a fuck about them, but you should because they are your family, Lorraine. And that counts for *something*. At least, it should. For somebody who claims to value the concept of family as much as you say you do, this shit should be obvious to you."

"Okay, Millie. Shit, I'll talk to her."

Chapter Eleven

The old neighborhood.

That's where the Langston family still lived. Rain had grown up around there in a house that she now owned. When she saw it was for sale, Rain bought it and had converted it into a safe house. It was just a few blocks from where she was standing. She took a second to wonder if she had known how close her mother's family was to that house, would she have reached out to them?

Knowing that the answer would have been no, Rain exhaled and tried to decide if this was really a door she wanted to open to her past.

You haven't given a shit about them all these years, so what the fuck are you doing here now?

Because Millie told you to take your black ass over here and not give her no argument, Rain thought and then laughed out loud.

"What?" Alwan asked.

"Nothing. I just thought of some funny shit."

"What was that?"

Rain looked at him.

"Never mind."

"Yeah, that's what I thought," Rain said and started for the house.

She had thought about giving Alwan her guns before she went inside.

Fuck that shit.

Although Millie assured her that her aunt Priscilla wasn't one of them, there were people on her mother's side of the family that believed that Jasper killed his wife, and they hated him for it. Keeping her weapons under those circumstances just seemed like the smart move.

When she got to the door, Rain stood there and asked herself one more time, despite what Millie said, if this was something that she wanted to do. She valued and respected the concept of family and what it meant to be a part of one. The family that she was a member of would do anything to help another member of The Family. Rain thought about Shy's story about the shoot-out that she got into with Jada West. Although Shy does an excellent job of playing nice, the truth was something else entirely.

That day, Shy had emptied her clip, killing one of their attackers, and dropped down to reload the plr22. When Jada turned to cover Shy, one of the attackers got a clear shot at Jada and shot her in the stomach. Shy slammed in the magazine, stood, and lit him up. When Black arrived at the scene, he found Jada holding her stomach, gasping for air, and Shy holding her.

"Stay with me, Jada," Shy said and looked up at Black.

He took a breath. "Get in the car, Cassandra."

"We can't just leave her."

Shy couldn't stand her ass, Rain thought. She could have just walked away and left her there to die. But Jada West was family. *So Shy put all that aside.*

This was her family, her *real* family. Rain rang the bell, stepped back, and waited. When the woman opened the door, Rain felt like she was looking at the only picture she had of her mother.

"Yes, can I help you?"

"Priscilla Langston?"

"Yes, I'm Priscilla Langston. Can I help you with something?"

"My name is Lorraine Robinson. Barbara Robinson was my mother."

"Oh my God, Lorraine?" Priscilla blinked a few times, and then she rushed toward Rain and hugged her. Hugged her so tightly that it made her feel uncomfortable. Although Millie said that she wasn't one of the people who hated her father, this wasn't the reception she was expecting. Rain expected her to be cordial, even friendly, but jovial and affectionate—no, she wasn't ready for this. But it felt good to her. It felt right, and Rain slowly put her arms around her aunt and hugged her.

"Oh my God, Lorraine, please come inside," she said, finally letting Rain go.

"Thank you," Rain said, and she stepped inside. Then she watched, almost spellbound, as Priscilla closed the door and turned to her. She looked so much like her mother.

"Let me have a look at you," she said and put on her glasses. "My God, Lorraine, you look just like Barbara when she was a little girl."

Rain frowned because all her life, she had been told that she looked like her father and had nothing of her mother. "Really?" she asked, not bothering to hide her disbelief.

"Sure do." Priscilla grabbed Rain's hand. "Come with me, Lorraine, and let me show you. I am *so* excited," she said and led Rain into her living room. "Have a seat." Aunt Priscilla pointed to the couch while she continued to the kitchen. "Can I get you something to drink, water or soda?" she paused. "I have tequila if you want something stronger."

Drinking tequila must run in the family. I wonder if she drinks Patrón too.

"No, ma'am. Water is fine, thank you," Rain said even though she wanted one. But since she was thinking about having the baby, she had decided not to drink.

While she waited for her aunt to return, Rain looked around the room at all of the pictures of family that filled the walls and zoomed in on one in particular. She stood up and walked to it. It was a picture of Priscilla and her mother on her wedding day. They both looked so beautiful, and her mother seemed so happy. As she continued to stare at the picture, the more Rain could see the resemblance with her mother that she had never seen before.

"She looked so beautiful that day," Priscilla said when she came into the living room with a glass of water and a photo album.

She sat down on the couch and patted the spot next to her. Rain took one last look at the picture and went to sit down as Priscilla flipped pages and was glad that she decided to do this. As for Priscilla, she was overjoyed that Barbara's baby girl was sitting next to her. She used to keep Rain all the time when she was a baby. Barbara would drop her off there, then go do what she needed to do with Eddie. One of the regrets she held was not keeping in touch with Rain and Miles, but Jasper would have none of that. That was why she stayed in touch with Millie. It wasn't much, but at least she could hear how they were doing. Priscilla happily continued to flip pages until she got to the one that she wanted Rain to see.

"There you are," she said and pointed. "See? You look like her." Priscilla handed Rain the album. "You got your daddy's complexion." She paused and looked at Rain before she said, "and his evil eyes." Then Priscilla gently touched Rain's face.

"But you got *her* soft, beautiful features. Her lips, her cheekbones, and her jawline. You get all that from your mother."

Hearing that made Rain smile.

"See? You look like your mama." Priscilla paused as Rain turned pages of the family she didn't know. There was something that she thought that she had to say. "I was sorry to hear that he suffered when he passed."

Rain looked at her. "Really?"

"Yes, Lorraine, I was. I don't know how much you know about what happened, but some people in our family were glad that he suffered and thought he got what he deserved. But I don't think anybody should suffer. Your father knows the truth of what he did, and he had to make his peace here on earth and before the Lord."

"I heard about what happened" was the only comment that Rain had, and then she thought about it. "Thank you for saying that," she said and turned the page. "This y'all?" she asked and pointed to a picture of teenagers that appeared to have been taken in that very room.

"That's us. That's your uncle Brayden. He's the oldest, and that's your aunt Charlene next to him. That's Vincent, Elliot, and Evangelia. They're twins. That's me, and that's your mother."

"She was the youngest?"

"She was the baby. And we looked out for her, and we all spoiled her, we did."

Rain closed the book and handed it back to Priscilla. "Thank you for showing me that."

"You're welcome, Lorraine." She put both hands on the book, exhaled, and looked at Rain. "It is really great to see you. I haven't seen you or Miles since you were kids. How is Miles?"

Now, it was Rain's turn to exhale, and she looked at Priscilla. "Miles is in jail." She paused and waited for a reaction, but Priscilla seemed unfazed. "Do you remember Jeff Ritchie?"

She frowned. "Of course, I remember that bastard. There are some people that you remember even when you try to forget."

"Miles killed him."

"I know. Millie told me. I was asking how he was doing in jail."

Rain laughed a little. "He's fine. I went out there to see him with his kids a couple of weeks ago."

Priscilla smiled excitedly. "I would like to meet Lakeda, Miles Junior, and Rasheeda one day. But one step at a time." She patted Rain's lap. "I'm just so glad that you're here in this house again after all these years."

"I've been here before?"

"This is the house we all grew up in, Lorraine. This is the first place your mama and daddy brought you when she came home from the hospital. When you were a baby, you were here every day. I used to keep you sometimes when your mother had something to do."

"I never knew that."

"I'm sure that there's a lot of things that Jasper didn't tell you about us." She opened the album and quickly turned to a page. "See?" Priscilla said, pointing to a picture of her mother holding Rain and surrounded by her sisters and brothers, and Evangelia was holding young Miles.

It made Rain feel that despite what she had come to believe her entire life, this *was* her family.

"Millie was telling me that you were worried about your daughter."

Priscilla closed her eyes and nodded slowly. "Your cousin, Sapphire." She flipped a few pages. "That's her."

"She's pretty."

"That's my baby girl. And, yes, I am worried about her. I haven't heard from her in a couple of weeks, and she's never gone this long without me hearing from her. I'm afraid something might have happened to her."

"You try calling her?" Rain asked and realized it was a stupid question.

"I called and left messages more times than I can count, sent texts, and I got no reply, and that is *not* like her. When I called her this morning, her phone was out of service."

"I see. You call the cops?"

"A week ago, and I haven't heard anything from them since."

"No surprise there."

"I knew it was a waste of time when I reported it."

"Where does she work?"

"She's a flight attendant. Sapphire's a very private person, so I'm not really all that sure if she still works there, but the last time we talked about it, she said it was a small private airline called Overseas Air . . . I think that's what it's called. Millie said that you might be able to help."

"I'll see what I can find out," Rain promised.

"Thank you, Lorraine. I appreciate whatever you can find out." She took Rain's hand and squeezed it. "Having you home means more to me than you know."

Chapter Twelve

"So," Diane said, "what's the plan for the day?"

"I thought we agreed that we would talk to Daniel Beason and Andrea Frazier. And then we were going to talk to Gayle and Albert separately."

"That's still the plan." Diane paused. "And then I have an appointment with Mike Black."

"You really think he's involved?"

"No."

"I was just checking." Jack paused and decided whether he wanted to ask his question. He sat up. "Then why are you going?"

"I'm interested in hearing his insights." Diane sat up and looked at him. "He's a killer, one that has never served a day for all the people he's murdered."

"He did get arrested for murdering his wife," Jack pointed out.

"Who was found alive, and I met her yesterday."

"And for kidnapping Congressman Spencer Horiwitz."

"Which got laughed out of court." She paused to see if Jack had anything else. "My point is Mike Black is a killer."

"And a damn good one."

"I want to know how a killer thinks," Diane said, but it was deeper than that.

"Want me to come along?"

"Not unless you just want to," she replied and got out of bed.

"Not especially," he said and followed her to the bathroom.

She turned on the shower. "I'll let you get in first, and I'll drive if you make me pancakes," she sang.

Jack shook his head. "Not falling for it, Diane. We are in separate cars today most of the day, and you know this," he said and turned around.

Diane laughed. "Where are you going?"

"To make you pancakes," Jack said and left the bathroom.

The first stop that Jack and Diane made that morning was at the home of Danial Beason and his wife, Susan. They parked in front of the Contemporary Craftsman-style home with its gabled roof, wide front porch, and pedestal-columned exterior finish with a blend of stone and wood.

"We are definitely in the wrong business," Diane said as they approached the house.

"We could quit the force and buy a bank."

"What would be the fun in that?" she asked and rang the bell.

"We might get robbed," Jack said and shrugged his shoulders as the door opened.

"Yes?" said the beautiful woman that answered the door, dressed in a pink Alaïa cashmere and silk pullover cropped top that showed off her 14K solid white gold navel ring, and Jimmy Choo Basette Mules adorned with exaggerated pearlescent baubles and delicate studs. "Can I help you?"

"Mrs. Susan Beason?" Diane asked, thinking that she was overdressed to be interviewed by the police about a murder.

"I'm Susan Beason."

"I'm Detective Mitchell, and this is my partner, Detective Harmon," Diane said, and they showed their badges. "We spoke on the phone yesterday."

Susan smiled. "Yes, Detectives, we've been expecting you. Please, come in," she said and stepped aside to allow the detectives into her home.

"Thank you for taking the time to see us, Mrs. Beason," Jack said as he and Diane stepped inside.

"We only have a few questions," Diane informed her.

Jack smiled at Susan. "I promise that we won't take up a lot of your time." Then his eyes drifted down to her navel.

"If there is anything that I can tell you that will help you catch whoever killed Elias, I have all the time you need," Susan said and led them into the huge, elaborately decorated living room where her husband was waiting. He was sitting on the couch, looking relaxed and comfortable. "Danny, this is Detective Mitchell and her partner, Detective Harmon."

Beason stood up to shake their hands. "Good morning, Detectives. Please, have a seat."

"Thank you for taking the time to see us, Mr. Beason. As *my* partner explained to your wife," Diane began with a tinge of jealousy in her voice because she saw how Jack was looking at Susan, "we only have a few questions, so we won't take up a lot of your time."

"Take as much time as you need, Detective. Anything that I can do to help," Beason said and sat down. Susan sat beside him and looped her arm in his.

"What can you tell me about Mr. Colton?" Jack asked, and once again, he and Diane were treated to another testimonial to what a wonderful husband and father Elias Colton was. A successful businessman and entrepreneur. A great man of vision who was a prominent leader in his community.

After asking a series of preliminary questions, Jack and Diane were ready to wrap things up and move on.

"Do you know anyone that might want to do him harm?" Diane asked.

"No, I can't say that I can," Beason answered.

"Everybody loved Elias," Susan said, and both Jack and Diane wondered if he had fucked her too.

After a few more questions, Jack and Diane stood up. "I think that's all we need for now," Diane said.

"If you think of anything," Jack stated, "no matter what it is, please, give me a call."

Mr. and Mrs. Beason got up and escorted the detectives to the door. "Anything you can think of would be helpful," Diane said on her way out the door.

When they got to Rockville Guaranty Savings and Loan to interview Andrea Frazier, her answers to those same preliminary questions were pretty much the same as they had just heard. "Prominent businessman and entrepreneur with a distinguished record of community service." She too had nothing but high praise for Elias Colton, humanitarian and pillar of the community.

"The man was a saint," Diane said when they walked out of the building. "If you overlook the multiple indiscretions, the man was a saint."

"*Alleged* multiple indiscretions."

"That's my next stop," Diane said, and Jack drove back to his apartment for her to pick up her car.

On the way there, she gave some thought to how she was going to handle Gayle. She had been told hy people that knew her that Gayle was bubbly, almost to the point of getting on your nerves.

Diane had decided to go straight at her and say, "Gayle Eager, you're under arrest for the murder of Elias Colton," and see where it took them. However, that plan went out the window when Gayle opened the door.

"Yes?" said the woman who answered the door, and Diane couldn't believe that it was the same woman that she had seen at the funeral. "Can I help you?"

"Mrs. Gayle Eager?"

"I'm Gayle Eager."

"I'm Detective Mitchell," Diane said and showed her badge. "We spoke yesterday."

"Yes, Detective. I've been expecting you. Please, come in," she said and stepped aside to allow the detective into her home.

Gayle Eager was dressed in a classically elegant black Carolina Herrera bracelet sleeve silk dress and Dolce & Gabbana leather stiletto pumps at the funeral. Her hair was styled in a chic, asymmetrical, comb-over peek-a-boo bob, and her face was flawlessly made up. Gayle also wore enough jewelry to make you take notice. That morning, she had on her 2009 World Series Championship Yankees sweats, her hair was pulled back in a short ponytail, and she wore no makeup.

"Thank you for taking the time to see me, Mrs. Eager," Diane said as she stepped inside. She also noticed that although her eyes weren't red, they were puffy as if she'd been crying.

That's what Visine is for, Diane thought.

"Can I get you something to drink? I just made a fresh pot of coffee," Gayle said and led Diane into the living room.

"I'd love some coffee, thank you."

"Just make yourself comfortable, and I'll be right back," Gayle said, but instead of having a seat in the living room and waiting, Diane followed her into the kitchen.

"I wanted to say how sorry I am for your loss. Everybody I've spoken with has told me what a good man that Elias Colton was," she said and sat down at the kitchen table.

"Thank you, Detective—"

"Diane," she said as Gayle reached into the cabinet for two coffee cups.

She turned to Diane and faked a smile. "Thank you, Diane. I learned a lot from Mr. Colton," she said as she filled Diane's cup.

"I understand that you and Mr. Colton were very close," Diane said, and Gayle's hand shook a bit as she poured her own. She put the pot down and glanced at Diane, who was looking directly at her.

"Yes," she said. Her voice cracked, and she avoided eye contact. "He mentored my husband

and me in our business." She handed the cup to Diane and sat down at the table with the detective. "We will both miss him and his guidance," Gayle said, staring into the cup as she stirred. When she looked up, Diane was still looking directly at her. Diane touched her hand softly.

"You were in love with him, weren't you, Gayle?" Diane asked, and Gayle started to cry.

She nodded her head, and the tears fell. "Yes," she said softly.

"Why don't you tell me what happened?"

Gayle didn't say anything. She just cried, and Diane let her go on for a while.

"You were there that night, weren't you?"

"Yes. But I didn't kill him."

"What happened, Gayle? I can help you if you tell me everything."

Gayle took a second or two to compose herself enough to say, "We were in love. He told Cissy it was over between them. He had filed for divorce. We were going to be together," she cried.

"What happened, Gayle?"

"I told Albert that I wanted a divorce."

"How'd he take it?"

"He got mad, said he was never gonna give me up." Gayle paused. "And he would kill any man that tried to take me from him. We argued, and I left the house."

"Where did you go?"

"I called Elias and told him that I told Albert, and he said to meet him at his place in midtown."

"So you went to the apartment. What time did you get there?"

"About seven."

"Building security said that Colton had no visitors that night. How did you get in without being seen?" Diane asked, even though she knew, but she wanted to see if the stories matched.

"Jonathan, that's the security guard, he wasn't there when I came in." She paused and thought about it. "He wasn't there when I left either."

"Does that often happen, the security guard not being at his post?"

"Elias said that it happened all the time, and he would complain to management about it. He told me that he was thinking about terminating his lease because of it."

"What time did you leave?"

"Around nine. But you have got to believe me. I didn't kill him, and he was alive when I left."

"Tell me everything that happened and everything that was said."

Gayle forced out a little laugh. "We didn't do much talking."

"I see." Diane exhaled. "So you two did the horizontal boogaloo, have a drink, and you leave. Then where did you go?"

"I went and checked into The Knickerbocker Hotel in Times Square, but we didn't have a drink."

"You didn't?" she asked in surprise.

"No. I have a severe intolerance to alcohol, so I don't drink."

That means somebody else was definitely there. "Did you see anybody when you left the building?"

"No. I just got in my car and drove to the hotel."

"What about your husband? Where was he? Do you know what he did after you left the house?"

"I don't know."

"Do you think that he could have followed you to Colton's that night?"

"I don't know."

"Did you tell him that it was Colton that you were leaving him for?"

Gayle looked horrified. "No. He would kill Elias," she said and then thought about it. *Could Albert have followed me and killed Elias?*

"Do you think he suspected that it was Colton that you were leaving him for?"

"I don't know. Maybe," she said softly. Until just then, she hadn't thought about it, but now she had to consider it.

"Do you think that your husband killed Elias Colton that night after you left there?"

Gayle looked at Diane for a few seconds. "I don't know. Maybe he did, but I just don't know."

When Diane drove away from the Eager home, she was surprised at how close her theory of the crime was to what actually happened. Except for them having an after-sex drink, she was right about most of it.

Don't pat yourself on the back just yet, she thought. They would still need to place Albert at the crime scene for her theory to turn into an arrest. So after dropping by The Knickerbocker Hotel and verifying that Gayle did indeed check in at nine twenty-nine, the detective headed to New Rochelle for her next appointment.

Chapter Thirteen

That morning, Mike Black sat in his office looking out the floor-to-ceiling window at the artificial lake, wishing that he was still in bed and was thinking about getting out of there and doing just that. He had been there since eight thirty preparing for a nine o'clock meeting with Meka to finalize the acquisition of a parcel of land in the Pocono Mountains. Although the meeting was over by ten thirty, he had made an appointment to speak with Detective Mitchell about Elias Colton's murder. Otherwise, he'd be back in the bed now with Shy. Her meeting with Reeva Duckworth didn't start until two that afternoon, so she kissed him good-bye and went back to sleep.

Now the question was, did Detective Mitchell really think he had anything to do with Colton's murder? He laughed each time he thought about it, but she was coming, so he needed to take it seriously. He did know Elias, and he was a criminal and a killer, as Shy pointed out. He didn't do it, nor did anybody in The Family, as far as he knew, but it wouldn't be the first time that a cop made a case out of nothing. Black was startled by his phone ringing. He looked at the display and saw that it was Erykah Morgan, the personal assistant that he shared with Meka.

"Yes, Erykah?"

"Bobby's here to see you."

"Send him in," Black said, and a few seconds later, Bobby came through the door.

"What's up, Mike?" Bobby said and walked to the bar to make a drink.

Black looked around his office. "Nothing. Absolutely nothing."

"Let's get the fuck up outta here then," Bobby said and shot his drink.

Black shook his head. "Can't. Got a meeting with Detective Mitchell."

"Ain't that the cop that Carmen saved?"

"The same."

"I never met her. What she look like?"

"She's worth a look."

"What does she want?"

"To talk about a murder."

"Who'd you kill?"

"Nobody."

"Then what does she want to talk about?"

"I know him, and I am a criminal."

Bobby laughed. "If I were a cop, I'd want to talk to you too."

"I guess that's why she's coming," Black said and yawned.

"You look tired."

"I was up late last night."

"What time did she come home?" Bobby asked, and Black looked surprised that he knew to ask. "What you looking at me like that for? I didn't just meet you." Bobby laughed. "You know, you're usually a smart guy, but even I wasn't stupid enough to buy Barbara a car when she was 16, no matter how much she whined and pouted about it."

"Two o'clock."

Bobby laughed. "I don't know what you're so worried about. She's gonna get fucked."

"Don't start, Bob. I don't wanna hear that shit."

"No, nigga. This payback is twenty-one years in the making. Remember when Barbara was born, and you used to tell me that shit all the time?" Bobby asked, laughing.

"I remember, and I still don't wanna hear that shit." Black smiled. "Unless you want to talk about all the pussy Brenda and Bonita are slinging at college."

Bobby stopped laughing. "I don't wanna hear that shit, Mike."

"Neither do I."

Bobby stood up. "It's just revenge for all the fathers' daughters we fucked."

"You outta here?"

"Yeah. What you doing after you talk to the cops?"

"Going home to bed."

"Holla at me when you wake up."

"Will do," Black said and watched Bobby leave his office.

When Bobby left, he was thinking about his girls. Bobby, like most men, had a traditional view of fatherhood. They were supposed to protect them from men like him and Black. *You remember what you were like,* he laughed about what he used to say.

Eighteen to eighty, blind, cripple, or crazy. Fat, funky, or ferocious, I don't care. They're getting fucked.

Although he did not doubt that Barbara was sexually active, he didn't want to think or hear about it. But Black had put something on his mind about Brenda and Bonita. My baby girls. He knew he had to let them grow up, let them date, let them experience life. Bobby had tried to keep a strong and close connection with his girls, giving them advice and trust that they would make good decisions.

"You going, Mr. Ray?"

"Yes, Lenecia, I have something to do." Bobby leaned on the counter. "But if I didn't, I would happily spend the rest of the day staring into your beautiful eyes and telling you fascinating stories fit for the world's most beautiful woman."

"You say the sweetest things to me," Lenecia said, smiling and thinking that she'd be down if he ever asked.

"I keep telling you, a few years ago, I would be a contender for your emotions," Bobby said and kept it moving toward the door because he could tell by the eager smile and the inviting eyes that he could have her with very little effort. "Have a good day, Lenecia," he said and held the door open for Diane.

"Good afternoon," Lenecia said, still smiling brightly over her flirtation with Bobby. "And welcome to Prestige Capital and Associates. How may I help you today?"

She took out her badge. "Detective Diane Mitchell to see Erykah Morgan."

"Yes, Detective. Erykah has been expecting you. If you wouldn't mind having a seat, I will let her know that you're here."

"Thank you," the detective said and went to sit down.

As soon as she was seated, the door opened, and in walked Reeva Duckworth dressed in an elegant red Chiara Boni La Petite Robe Serin dress with a one satin notch lapel.

"Hey, Reeva," Lenecia said.

"Hey, girl. Can't talk. Got a meeting with Mrs. Black to prepare for," Reeva said as she passed the desk. It raised an eyebrow on the detective because she didn't know that Shy worked there too. "But call me, and we'll grab drinks after work."

After that, the detective's wait wasn't long, and soon, Erykah was escorting Diane through the halls at Prestige to the office of Mike Black. He stood up when Erykah showed her in.

"Good afternoon, Detective Mitchell."

"Hello, Mr. Black."

"Please, have a seat," he said and extended his hand toward the chairs in front of his desk.

"Thank you."

"Can I get you anything?" Erykah asked.

"No, I'm fine."

"Thank you, Erykah," Black said, and she closed the door on the way out.

"Thank you for seeing me," Diane said and sat in front of the desk.

"Not a problem."

Diane smiled. "I missed you at Carmen's wedding."

"But I didn't miss you."

"You were there? I didn't see you," she paused. "And neither did Carmen."

"Oh, but I *was* there. I didn't stay for the reception, but I was there. I wouldn't miss Carmen's wedding for anything in the world," Black said, thinking about Shy's reaction when he told her that Carmen was getting married and Jada was going to be her maid of honor.

Carmen . . . and Jada. And you're going. Shy shook her head. *Not without me.*

"She kept saying that you were there." Diane laughed. "She said she could feel it."

"I was there. I thought that you and Jada looked very nice in those off-the-shoulder champagne mermaid bridesmaid gowns the two wore."

"I would have sworn you weren't there," Diane said, thinking what that said about her observation skills. "Anyway."

"I know that you came here to interrogate me, but before we get started, do you really think that I had anything to do with Elias's murder?"

"No, I don't. And, yes, I could have asked the only real question that I have for you while we were standing outside of Saint Luke's."

"Which is?"

"Can you tell me where you were on the night that Elias Colton was murdered?" Diane asked.

"I was home with my wife, my mother, my mother-in-law, two of my three children, and six bodyguards." Black paused, and Diane braced herself for what he was going to say next: "My daughter, Michelle, just turned 16, so she was out in her new car," Black said because that was the most important thing that happened that night. Then he reached for the phone. "If you like, I could call and have the security footage from that night made available to you."

Diane laughed. "I don't think all that is necessary, but I appreciate the offer to be so transparent," she said, knowing that she would take him up on that offer if the investigation called for it.

"So why are you here?"

"I already told you. I am very interested in hearing your insights. And I don't mean you any disrespect, but you're a killer, and I need to be able to think like a killer."

"It will make you a better cop," Black laughed. "So you want me to be . . . what? A murder consultant?"

"Sort of." And then she confidently said, "Yes."

"Why me?"

"Despite the fact that you're a killer, two of the most important people in my life have immense respect for you. I need to understand why that is for my own reasons. And on top of that, you're the best-qualified person I know."

"I understand why Carmen likes you, and Jack has so much respect for you." Black paused to think carefully about the request that she was making of him. "I'll think about it, Detective."

"That is all I can ask," Diane said, stood up, and was about to thank him for his time and consideration when she decided, since she was there, to seek his insight. "Who do *you* think killed Elias Colton?"

"Albert and Gayle look good for it, but you think it's deeper than that." Black stood up. "If you don't, you should."

"Why is that?" Diane asked on the way out of the office, and Black laughed.

"Just a feeling," he said, thinking, *Albert is too big a pussy to kill Elias.* Erykah stood up when they came out of the office. "I will think about what you asked, Detective. Erykah will show you out."

"Thank you for taking the time to see me."

"My door is always open to you."

"Some may take that as you accepting my proposal."

"I understand why Carmen likes you. Have a good day, Detective Mitchell."

"You too, Mr. Black," Diane said, and Erykah escorted her out of the building. When she got in the car, Diane called Jack. He had talked to Albert.

"At first, he denied everything, but then he admitted that he suspected that they were having an affair, and he followed her to the building, but he said that he didn't go in because security was there when he got there, so he went home."

"I don't buy it, Jack," Diane said as she drove away from Prestige. "If he followed her straight there, and Jonathan wasn't there when she went in, why is that he wasn't there when Albert got there?"

"Bad timing?"

"Or he's lying, and he went in right behind her," Diane said, but then she thought about what Black said.

Albert and Gayle look good for it, but you think it's deeper than that. If you don't, you should.

Chapter Fourteen

Now that his meeting with Detective Mitchell was over and he had nothing else to do, Black closed his laptop and headed for the door. He had just told Erykah that he was gone for the day when he saw Meka, the CEO of the company. Her door was open, and then he heard voices. Black went to the door and stuck in his head.

"Morning, ladies," he said to Meka and Gladys Gordan, head of the entertainment division, two women that loved to talk.

"Morning, Mike," Gladys replied.

"Join us if you got a minute," Meka said, waving him in.

"I was just on my way somewhere," Black said as he came and sat down.

"We were talking about the next season of *The Breakout* and who's going to host it," Meka told him.

The Breakout was a television reality series where up-and-coming artists competed for a chance at a recording contract from Big Night

Records, which was a part of the entertainment division at Prestige. Black's sister, Scarlet, hosted the last season, whose relentless pursuit of musical perfection drove last season's crop of contestants to either quit or get voted off the show.

"What's wrong with Scarlet?" he asked.

"She said she's not sure if she wants to do it this season," Gladys replied.

"Scarlet has a lot going on in her world with La Soufrière erupting on the island," Black said of the volcano that erupted on the island of St. Vincent. "Count her out."

"You sure?" Meka asked.

"No, not at all. I mean, the show is hers if she wants to do it, but I don't think, with all that's going on in her world, that she will. So we should have somebody in place and ready to go if she says no. That just makes sense."

"You're right," Gladys said, and Meka was glad that he saved her the trouble of saying it because before Black walked in and joined them, Gladys wasn't moving in that direction. She was insisting that Scarlet had to do it.

Funny how that works, Meka smiled.

"So, who do you have in mind?" Black asked.

"That's the other problem," Meka said.

"What's that?"

"We're short on hosts for the show," Gladys said.

"What about Cristal?" Black asked of the label's top seller.

She had hosted the show's first three seasons when the original project, a movie about a woman getting her break in the music industry, was canceled when it was discovered that Cristal couldn't act. She was terrible, but it was the outtake footage of her verbally abusing the film crew that the show's original concept was born. Each week, Cristal verbally abused the acts to the point where some quit before she either kicked them off the show or the viewers voted off.

"She's going on tour in Europe with Mia Rubio," Meka said, and Black snapped his fingers and pointed at Gladys.

"I'm supposed to tell you that you're wrong for that."

Gladys looked at him strangely, and Meka smiled because she agreed with Michelle. When she called the next day to complain, the boss's daughter was transferred to Meka.

"What am I wrong for?"

"Michelle said that you wrong for letting Roselyn Pierce win when you know Mia should have."

"I had already planned on signing Mia. I just put her on the show to give her more exposure for her debut. Mia got the most votes, and Roz would have been the runner-up. That way, I got to sign both of them. It was just business." Gladys giggled it off, but they had gotten plenty of mail about how Mia should have won.

"That's what I said, and she said to tell you that you're wrong for that." Black laughed. "I've been meaning to tell you that for the longest."

Gladys frowned. "Well, what do you think?"

"I think it's your division, and you run it the way you see fit."

"Which is what I told her, Mike," Meka chimed in.

"But do you think that I was right?" Gladys asked.

"How's Mia's single doing?" Black asked to answer her question.

"It's number seven on Billboards Hot R&B and Hip-Hop chart and thirty-eight on the Hot 100."

"There's your answer," Black said, and Gladys smiled a satisfied smile. "Who's producing Roselyn Pierce's album?"

"Paul," Meka dropped.

Black held up his hand. "You're letting P produce?" he asked of Paul "P Harlem" Roberts, Big Night Records' other top moneymaker. Meka nodded, and they both looked at Gladys.

"How do you tell Paul no?" she asked meekly, and that sent the conversation in an entirely different direction that continued for the next hour and a half.

It was going on one o'clock when Black told Lenecia to have a nice day. But before he left,

Gladys and Meka Black had got Cristal on Zoom and asked her to host the show when she returned from Europe if Scarlet didn't want to. She agreed because how do you say no to Mike Black?

He knew when he got in the Escalade with William that it was too late. The whole point of leaving was to get back in bed with Shy. Black was proven right when he walked into their bedroom. Shy had finished her hair and makeup and was getting dressed.

"Hi."

"What are you doing here?" Shy asked and put on the Proenza Schouler white blazer with a trio of mixed buttons and matching flared pants.

"I came to get back in the bed with you."

"You're a little too late for that."

"I see," he said, walking up behind Shy and helping her put on the Pomellato rose gold and diamond pendant. "I was trying to get out of there—"

"But you stopped and talked to . . ."

"Meka and Gladys."

Shy sat down on the bed. "I'm surprised you're here," she said and put on a pair of Alaïa perforated leather sandals.

"I got them to a certain point, and then I left," Black said as Shy stood up and got her Fendi Sunshine Canvas Bag.

"You still getting back in the bed?" she asked on her way to the door.

"I'm gonna lie down for a while, and then I'm gonna go holla at Bobby."

Shy stopped and turned toward him. "No, you're not. You *and your* daughter are going to be here when I get back," she said, leaned in, and kissed his lips. "You should have skipped the meeting and come home." Shy kissed him again and started for the door. "Be home when I get here."

It was twenty minutes later when Chuck parked in Shy's space at Prestige Capital and Associates, and she went inside for her meeting with Reeva Duckworth. Although her business, CAMB Overseas Importers, operated independently of Prestige, there was more than enough room in the building for Shy's small staff.

"Good afternoon, Mrs. Black," Lenecia said. "How are you today?"

"I'm fine, Lenecia. How are you?"

"Doing great," she said as the phone rang. She waved to Shy. "Prestige Capital and Associates, how may I direct your call?" she said as Shy went to her office.

CAMB Overseas Importers was only an idea that Shy was fooling around with until she met Cebrián Sandalio, an associate of Rodrigo Iñíguez, who Black was reluctantly involved with. He handed her a piece of his profitable US Medicinal and Pharmaceutical products import business. After that, she negotiated a deal to import women's apparel from Honduras when she ran into Carlo DeSalice, another of her husband's associates. He turned Shy onto Cerasuolo Milazzo, an Italian apparel manufacturer looking for a new US distributor, and her business took off after that.

"Hey, everybody," Shy said when she came in and headed for her office. On the way, she stuck her head in Reeva's door. "Hey, Reeva. You busy?"

"Just chatting with Patty."

"Who's Patty?"

"She's helping me get this printer connected to the internet."

"Oh, okay. Stop by my office when you get done," she said and went on to her office.

Later that day, they had a meeting with Óscar Acosta to export handcrafted furniture and bedding to Honduras, which she was importing from Italy. As she prepared for the meeting, Shy thought about what she was going to say to Michelle. One thing was sure . . . She was taking the car away, and she didn't care what Black said.

"You wanted to see me, Shy?"

"Yes. Come in and have a seat," she said, and Reeva sat down. "I saw you at Elias Colton's funeral. I didn't know that you knew him."

"Yes, I knew him. I didn't know that you and Mr. Black knew him."

"Michael is a member of the Association of Black Businesses."

"I didn't know that either," Reeva laughed a little. "I used to work for Elias at Titanium Distributing Service when I first graduated from college."

"I didn't know that."

"It was on my résumé."

"I barely read your résumé. I hired *you,* not your résumé."

When Reeva arrived at the office for the interview, Shy was hungry, so they went to lunch and talked over their meal. Shy was so impressed that she hired her before dessert.

"Good to know." Reeva paused, feeling good about what Shy said. "I had a friend that worked at Titanium as the shipping manager, and she brought me in as an entry-level shipping clerk. But she hated it, and I used to wonder why because I loved my job. The people, the work environment were great. But not her. She hated it and was looking for the door. So when she quit, her assistant took over, and he couldn't handle the job. Most of the time, it was me covering up his mistakes. He lasted about six months before he was fired. But apparently, Elias had been watching how I was doing my job and his job, and I was promoted to shipping manager."

"How'd you like it?"

"I quit less than two years later."

"It's different when you're actually in the job. What made you quit?"

Not wanting to speak ill of the dead, Reeva said, "The environment had changed."

It had changed from a nurturing culture that promoted collaborations and fostered growth to one where she was sexually harassed almost daily by Elias and several of the other managers.

"That's all I wanted, Reeva," Shy said, and Reeva stood up.

"All right then, I'm gonna get ready for our meeting."

"Óscar Acosta should be here soon," Shy said, and Reeva left her office.

Chapter Fifteen

Quentin Hunter sat in his office at Innovative Investments, trying to muster up the courage to pick up the phone. After graduating from Howard, where he met and was roommates with Daniel Beason, he returned to Houston. There, he began his business career as an accountant, with a focus on real estate accounting. He was hired as a junior development associate at Pearland Real Estate Development Company. He communicated with clients throughout projects, developing budgets, lining up vendors and contractors, conducting market research, and working on financial models.

With the experience that he gained, Quentin became a real estate broker and put his first deal together. The project costs were just over $10 million, which would be financed with 30 percent equity and 70 percent debt. That meant Quentin would need to come up with around $3 million, and since he didn't have that on hand, he recruited investors. Now that he had access to cash, Quentin acquired the property to build on, developed the plan, and got approval from the local government before breaking ground.

During those years, Quentin had the good fortune to meet Hadley Abraham, the son of New York real estate mogul Tweed Abraham, and the two young investors became fast friends. Quentin took full advantage of the opportunity to invest along with Hadley. After working on a few projects in the Houston area, the pair moved on to Vegas, Los Angeles, and Miami and made millions. By the age of 38, in addition to substantial holdings in the markets, Quentin owned a portfolio of apartments and hotels, as well as commercial and industrial properties nationwide. Now, at 52, he was looking for a new challenge in business.

But what he was thinking about had nothing to do with business. This was personal. He hadn't stopped thinking about her since the second that he saw her. And when she spoke, not only did her voice blow his mind, but also she had something to say. Once they were left alone that night, Quentin extended his hand, inviting her out on the balcony to talk. They looked out at the spectacular view of the Long Island Sound and spoke for over an hour. It had been awhile since he had a conversation like that, and she was so beautiful. Quentin picked up her card, surprised that he hadn't memorized the number as many times as he'd sat and simply stared at it, then reached for the phone.

"Here goes," he said aloud and dialed.

"Good morning. Pearson MDS General Contracting, how may I direct your call?" Kaloni asked.

"May I speak with Ebony Maddox, please."

"Your name, sir?"

"Quentin Hunter."

"Yes, Mr. Hunter. Would you please hold?"

"Thank you," he said and was treated to smooth jazz until Ebony's melodic voice came on the line and poured into his ear.

"Good morning, Quentin. How are you today?"

"Doing just fine, thank you. And what about you? How are you this morning?"

"I'm awesome. Busy, as always, but awesome."

"Then I won't take up a lot of your time." He took a breath. "I was wondering if you had decided whether you were going to join the association or not, and if you do, would you be interested in working with me on the grant-writing team for the fundraiser? I think your legal skills would be a good fit."

"Yes, I did join." Ebony smiled since she knew where this conversation was going. Quentin had called to ask her out and was using the association as cover. She thought it was sweet, so she happily played along. "I joined that night, and thank you so much for inviting me. I can see how being a member of the association would be good for my firm."

"It was my pleasure. I'm glad you saw the value in it."

"Yes, definitely. But as interesting as the grant-writing team is—"

"And exciting, don't forget that," Quentin joked and prepared to be let down.

"And exciting. Can't forget that," Ebony giggled. "But as soon as I said that I wanted to join, Elaine immediately assigned me to her administrative staff as part of her legal team," Ebony said. Quentin correctly assumed that since Elaine never said no to anything he asked, that Black had something, if not *everything*, to do with Ebony's assignment to the administrative legal team on her first day as a member. So now it was time for the direct approach. *I should have led with that anyway.*

"Well then, if that's the case, I guess I'll just have to drop the pretense and ask you if you would have dinner with me tonight?"

"I would love to have dinner with you, Quentin," Ebony said, and he got excited but kept his composure like he expected her to say yes.

"That's great." He paused to breathe. "Have you ever been to The Musket Room?"

"I have not. Why don't you text me the address, and I'll meet you there at eight. Sound good?"

"Sounds good."

"Great. I'm looking forward to it, but I do have to go. I have a million things to do today so that I can be on time to have dinner with you." She paused and dropped her voice an octave. "And you *do* want me to be on time, don't you?"

"I do. I really do." *I want you right now,* he thought. "So I'll let you go."

"You have an awesome day, and I'll see you tonight," Ebony said, hung up the phone, and got back to work.

Ebony spent most of the day working with Marvin and the accountant, Dominica Paris, on the underground exfiltration system for stormwater and the new sanitary system for the 12,000-square-foot community center project that Pearson MDS had been awarded the contract to build. It was getting late in the evening, too late to go home and change for her date with Quentin, so she would have to go with the wintergreen Lafayette 148 New York dress and button-up jacket that she had on. Ebony gathered her things, turned out her light, and headed out for the evening. She had been looking forward to it all day because she enjoyed his company.

"Good night, Marvin," Ebony said as she passed his office on her way out.

When he didn't answer, Ebony stopped, came back, and looked in on him. She had noticed that Marvin had seemed sad, distracted at times during the day, and now he was just sitting there with a blank look on his face.

"Marvin?"

"Huh?" he said and looked up.

"You all right?"

"Yeah, I'm fine," he said and quickly began moving some papers around on his desk.

"You *sure* you're all right? You've been a little distracted today."

"It's nothing. I'm fine, really. I just got a lot on my mind." He stood up and walked to the door. "You go have a good time, and we'll talk in the morning," he said and walked her to the elevator.

"All right then, if you're OK."

"I'm fine," he said as the door opened, and Ebony got on the elevator. "We'll talk in the morning."

"Good night, Marvin," she said as the doors closed.

Marvin went back to his office and got ready to leave. He sat down to turn off his computer, thinking that Ebony was right. He had been distracted with thoughts of how Sataria used him to kill Serek and how that broke his heart. Therefore, to ease his pain, he was fucking Joslin. He picked up the phone and called her cell.

"Hey, Money," she answered when he called.

"I'm getting ready to leave. Why don't you meet me at the hotel?"

"I'm here waiting for you," she giggled. "I never left. Good as that dick is, I may never leave this room."

"See you in a little while," Marvin said, turned off his computer, and went to meet her.

The Musket Room on Elizabeth Street billed itself as a modern take on homestyle New England cooking served in a rustic-chic environment. It was the place where Quentin had arranged to meet Ebony. He hadn't thought about much else other than having dinner with her since he hung up the phone. Quentin looked around for Ebony and then approached the maître d'.

"Good evening, sir, and welcome to The Musket Room."

"Quentin Hunter. I have reservations for two."

Once the maître d' said that their table wasn't ready, Quentin was escorted to the bar, ordered a drink, and waited for Ebony to arrive. For the first time in years, a woman had him nervous. So he tried to stay busy before the date and hit the gym for a sort of predate workout. As date-time approached, he took a shower and then listened to some music while picking out something comfortable to wear. When Quentin was dressed and ready to go, he took a minute to relax with a glass of wine. He planned to have fun with Ebony. He'd thought of a few topics to talk about in advance. In his mind's eye, Ebony was the most beautiful woman he had ever seen, and that beauty carried over into her personality. So he was going to try hard not to fuck it up.

When their table was ready, the maître d' escorted him there, and Quentin waited impatiently for Ebony's arrival as eight o'clock came . . . and went without incident.

She's not coming.

Under different circumstances, he'd be the first one to tell you that he was tripping, agonizing over what to wear and what to say to her . . . thinking about how aggressive to be or if he should be aggressive at all. Being aggressive and going after what he wanted had served him well in the past, but for some reason, Quentin felt like Ebony was different from the women he dated since Leslie, his first wife, left him. Too many of the women he'd met since then were interested in him for what he could do for them. Being with Ebony felt like it wasn't about his money, and that was a refreshing change.

At eight twenty-three, a hostess escorted Ebony to the table where Quentin anxiously awaited. He stood up when he saw her coming, overjoyed that she was standing in front of him.

"I'm sorry to have kept you waiting, Quentin," Ebony said as the hostess pulled out the chair for her, and she sat down.

"It's all right. You're here now. And, fortunately, you were worth the wait. You look incredible tonight."

"Thank you very much, Quentin. You're looking very handsome yourself."

"Thank you," he said and allowed himself to get a little excited. *Maybe she really is digging you, old man,* he thought.

"And I'm sorry to be so late getting here. After I left the office, I realized that I had left some papers I needed for a meeting in the morning, so I had to go back for them. You forgive me?" she asked.

"Only if you promise me that you will be a fascinating dinner conversationalist."

"It's a deal," she said, picking up her menu as their server approached the table.

"Can I bring you something from the bar, sir?"

"Glenfiddich, straight up." He looked at Ebony. Her eyes were driving him insane.

"And the lady will have?"

"I'll have a Mai Tai, please."

The server took our order for dinner, Glory Bay Salmon with potatoes and black truffles for Ebony and the Lamb Shank with roasted baby beets for Quentin. After their server left the table, there was a brief moment of silence as Quentin stared into Ebony's eyes, and she smiled in response.

"So, how are you tonight, Quentin?" she said, finally breaking the silence.

"I'm doing fine tonight."

"I wanted to say again how sorry I am about your friend," Ebony said as their server returned with their drinks.

"Thank you, Ebony. Elias was a good man, a good friend. You don't get too many people in your life that you can say that about."

"Do the police know or have any clue who did it."

"Not that I know of. I talked to the detectives assigned to his case. They asked me a bunch of questions like they thought I did it, but they were pretty tight-lipped when it came to answering *my* questions," he said, chuckling. "I know that they questioned Mike at the funeral."

Ebony laughed. "Did they really?"

"Right outside the church." He chuckled. "I'm sure Mike is used to that kind of thing happening all the time."

"I wouldn't know," Ebony was very careful to say.

Ebony knew that Quentin knew Black. Knew him well enough for Black to invite him to Michelle's birthday party, but did that mean he knew anything about The Family and its activities? She didn't know, and therefore, commenting further was not going to happen. But one thing was sure . . . Ebony did like Quentin. He was an intelligent man, and she had enjoyed the time that they'd spent together. In addition, she thought that Quentin was a very handsome man, *sexy as hell*. So she felt that she should take some time to get to know the man who was trying to get to know her.

"So tell me, who is Quentin Hunter? What's behind the image you present to the world?"

"What do you want to know?"

"Who you are."

"Let's see. I was born and raised in Houston, and I went to Howard and got a degree in accounting." He paused and thought about his list of prepared topics, glad to be getting the résumé portion of the evening out of the way early. He would much rather talk about her. "After that, I came back to Houston and started my career as a real estate accountant."

"So you define yourself by what you do?"

"No . . . well—yeah, I guess we all kind of do."

"We do."

"So who are *you*, Ebony?"

She laughed. "I'm a lawyer."

"See," Quentin said, and they shared a laugh as their cocktails were served.

Chapter Sixteen

It was just about that time when Marvin arrived at the hotel where he'd been staying since he walked out on Sataria. He felt numb, like someone punched him in the stomach and then straightened him up with an upper shot to the jaw.

Numb.

That was how he'd felt every day since Cleavon dropped the bomb on him that Sataria got him and his friend, Alphonse, to kill her first husband just like she had gotten him to kill her second husband, Serek. He didn't want to believe that Sataria could use him like that. But after Cleavon played the recording of her saying, *I can get that man to do anything I want him to do for me,* he couldn't deny it. Sataria had violated his trust, lied to him, and it hurt.

And I loved her.

What was most devastating was that she wasn't who or what he thought her to be. Marvin had muscled his way into Serek's company, Pearson Construction, after Serek came to him needing to borrow $50,000 to make payroll and cover expenses until he got a draw down from the general contractor. Since Marvin didn't have the money, he planned to get it from Judah, but he happened to see his father first.

Nick told him to tell Judah that he didn't need the money and that he would stake him. But instead of the fifty thousand he'd asked for, Nick told Marvin to give Serek $100,000. "And this is how you're gonna handle him," Nick said. Then he took him to school. He had run this game dozens of times, and Nick told Marvin precisely what to say to Serek when he met with him. Marvin listened like a student to what Nick said, and when he finished, Marvin was excited about the prospects.

"Then you have two choices. Either you own a construction company, or you'll make money driving him into bankruptcy."

The next afternoon, at exactly one o'clock, Marvin arrived at Pearson Construction, and that is when Sataria got his attention. She was beautiful, with brown skin, sexy, slanted eyes, and full lips that complemented her exquisite figure.

Now, she is outstanding. Big-ass titties and long legs that lead to hips and an ass that I'd enjoy squeezing while I take my time fucking her long and hard, Marvin thought the second he saw her. He knew that he had her attention too when she showed up at The Four Kings a few nights later.

At the meeting, Marvin laid it all out for Serek.

"Call it an investment . . . in your business. That makes us partners."

When Serek told him that he wasn't interested in having a partner, Marvin explained that he was interested in the money because the last thing he needed was to default on the job. But on the other hand, having him as a partner would be much more beneficial. Serek would have an unlimited source of capital to fund future projects.

"And I have access, and more importantly, I have influence. With that access and that influence, I would be able to put us on to bigger contracts."

After that, Serek was all in.

And it wasn't all that long after that when Sataria's visits to The Four Kings became more frequent. Sataria made it obvious from the start that she was interested in Marvin, and he was interested in being with her. The flirtation between the two was intense, but it was months before they became lovers. Despite how they met and the sizzling-hot affair they engaged in, Sataria presented herself as a virtuous, moral woman, and that is how Marvin thought of her. He fell in love with her—only to find out that she had somebody kill her first husband and then got him to do the same.

"And I loved her," he said aloud. "How could she have done that to me—to us?"

It hurt.

And that led to anger.

It was hard for him not to react to his anger when Sataria came to the office to explain herself the day after he walked out on her. Marvin fought off his inclination to retaliate, to hurt the person who hurt him.

"Please talk to me," she pleaded, but those pleas fell on deaf ears.

"I am so mad at you right now that I can't think straight."

"I understand."

"So before I say something I'll regret, I need some space to process this," Marvin said. But she had violated his trust, and knowing that she could hurt and betray him, he knew it was over between them.

"I understand. I just want to say that I'm sorry, and I hope that you give me a chance to explain," she said that day. "I love you," Sataria said and left Marvin feeling overwhelmed by intense and conflicting emotions that he was unable to make sense of.

His solution was to avoid the experience altogether by engaging in what was known as avoidance behaviors. A way to release his anger, a physical release to escape from emotion, and for Marvin, that was Joslin. And she was all for it.

"It's only fair since you killed my man."

He met Joslin Braxton when Black told Jackie that he wanted to know how Kojo's organization was set up, and she sent Marvin and Baby Chris to hit the streets and ask questions. They'd heard from Chee-Chee and Zach that their problem with Kojo was named Waylon. And as it turned out, Waylon was Kojo's problem as well. Joslin was Waylon's woman. Marvin had met her at Pago's when he and Baby Chris were there looking for him. She had seen Marvin once before at Club Constellation when he threw Lian Johnson on a table next to the one where Joslin was sitting.

"Oh shit," she shouted when the table broke.

It excited her.

Marvin excited her.

Then one night when she was mad at Waylon, Joslin came to Conversations looking for Marvin and thinking about grudge fucking. As it happened that night, Marvin was angry with Sataria too. So when he was alerted to her presence in the club, he had her escorted to the gambling room. They talked, had a few drinks, Marvin told her that he was interested in her, and then Joslin explained herself.

"I'm just another woman with a thing for bad boys." Joslin sipped her drink. "Fine ass, sexy-ass bad boys like you, Money. What you're interested in is fucking me."

"Would that be cool?"

"Yes, because for real—for real, I'm seriously interested in fucking you," Joslin said, and she emptied her glass.

"I think we should do something about that," Marvin replied and left Conversations with Joslin. They went to the nearest hotel.

However, when Marvin wasn't totally focused on something else, be it work or fucking Joslin, the sadness of the loss of the relationship he had, or at least the one he *thought* he had, would settle in. He would think about the good things in their relationship that he would miss. However, Sataria had shattered his trust, and Marvin wondered if he would ever completely trust a woman again. He had never loved a woman the way that he loved Sataria.

"You didn't know what love was until you met Sataria," he said and unlocked the door.

As soon as the door closed, Joslin moved closer to him, and he put his arms around her, and they kissed. He enjoyed the feeling of sheer ecstasy as her hands explored his body, and it made his dick stiffen. While they kissed, his tongue was pushing its way into her mouth as they got caught up in the moment. Joslin stopped in front of the bed, and he ran his tongue across the blue bra trimmed in white lace that hugged her succulent breasts. His heart beat a little faster as she slowly and seductively uncovered her breasts, and he saw her plump, chocolate nipples. Marvin stood back and watched her closely as she allowed each piece to fall to the floor.

Once she was naked, she gazed into his eyes, and Marvin squeezed her breasts softly, caressed them, loved them with both of his hands, all the while thoroughly enjoying the sweet taste of her tongue in his mouth. Then Marvin took her nipple into his mouth and began sucking it greedily, rolling it around in his mouth. She grabbed and held his head there until she had to push his head away because it made her want to feel him inside her.

Joslin unbuttoned his shirt and ran her hands over his chest. Marvin watched as her tongue moved softly across his chest. The sensation of her tongue flicking his nipple made his entire body quiver. She unbuckled his pants and gently pushed him onto the bed. She couldn't remember ever wanting a man this badly.

Joslin sashayed her naked body over to the bed, and his hands roamed freely across her flesh. Marvin took her breasts, held them, squeezed them, and ravished them with his tongue. She ran her hands all over his body and then knelt before him. Then she lay across the bed with her legs spread open as if she were inviting him in. Joslin kissed him passionately, stroking his erection, and put a condom on him. Marvin pulled her on top of him. She wiggled her hips and moved her body slowly until she had adjusted herself to his size.

It felt so good, him sliding in and out of her that she didn't want him to stop. Joslin moved her body from side to side, rubbing her nipples across his, and Marvin was ecstatic. He grabbed her ass and ran his hands up and down her back and across her cheeks. Then she started to move her hips faster.

"I'm coming!" she yelled, and her head drifted back.

Marvin felt his dick expand. He pushed it to her harder. Then he felt her body begin to shake. Joslin moved her body up and down on him, grinding her hips into him with each stroke. As Joslin drenched him with her juices, Marvin slid his hands from her shoulders, down her back, and then he gripped her beautiful, firm ass. Joslin leaned forward and kissed him while she continued to ride him until she made him come hard inside her.

"That was good," Joslin said as she got out of bed and went into the bathroom. When she was dressed and ready to leave for the club, she had a question. "Can I see you tomorrow?"

"I'll call you."

Joslin kissed him and then let herself out, thinking, *You gonna want some more of this, Money.*

Chapter Seventeen

The FBI's White-Collar Crimes division investigated criminal activities like public corruption, money laundering, securities and commodities fraud, bank and financial institution fraud, and embezzlement, targeting sophisticated, multilayered fraud cases that harm the economy. Corporate fraud was one of the FBI's highest criminal priorities. In addition to causing significant financial losses to investors, corporate fraud had the potential to cause immeasurable damage to the US economy and investor confidence.

That morning, Special Agent Connie Lewis, whose specialty was cases that involved accounting schemes designed to deceive investors, auditors, and analysts about the actual financial condition of a corporation or business entity, had just finished up the paperwork on a guilty plea to the charge of Grand Larceny in the Fourth Degree, in violation of New York Penal Law. Now, she could turn her attention to the failure of Emerson Savings and Loan and the sale to Daniel Beason. Once Connie had all her ducks in a row, she went to meet with her supervisor.

"Regulators found substantial losses which made them question the solvency of the bank," she said to Simon Kats, the supervisor of Criminal Investigations.

"What type of losses are we talking about here, Connie?"

"An unpaid final judgment and a deficiency balance following a foreclosure of collateral."

"And the results of the audit were?"

"The audit found the bank was making unsound loans and noted that if paper losses were realized, the savings and loan would be insolvent."

"Has your team identified what led to the insolvency?"

"The bank failure was caused by poor risk management decisions and bad loans. When credit standards were lowered, it created severe problems for the bank because it was too heavily invested in nonbank activities with real estate investment trusts that resulted in huge losses."

"Nothing new there, Connie," he said, but he knew that she was going somewhere.

He had recruited the lawyer-turned-FBI agent personally because of her ability to objectively evaluate information, analyze legal issues, and communicate them to him clearly. She just liked to take her time and slowly build the case for what she wanted to do. But there were certainly times when Kats wished she'd skip the buildup and get right to the point.

"When interest rates rose, it reduced demand for real estate investment trusts. In that environment, investors typically opt for safer income plays, such as US Treasuries, but they were weighed down by their investment in suburban malls, which, by that time, were in decline, to pivot to something safer."

"Which is why it was eventually seized by federal regulators and put into receivership," Kats said, attempting to move her along.

"Our investigation found connections between the failure of Emerson Savings and Loan and the sale to Daniel Beason. I want to explore his involvement in Rockville Guaranty Savings and Loan and The Green Ridge Development Corporation."

"I've always trusted your instincts in the past. No point in stopping now."

"Thank you, sir."

"You are authorized to proceed with this phase of your investigation. Make recommendations concerning any criminal prosecution, civil, or administrative proceedings that you deem appropriate. And, Connie, please, keep me informed of the progress."

"Don't I always?" she said and stood up.

"When it suits your purpose, yes," Kats said as Connie left his office.

Now that she had the go-ahead to move against Daniel Beason, the first thing on her agenda was to have Harrison Davis, the former CEO of National Savings Life, brought in for a chat. He was recently found guilty of one count of wire fraud for soliciting more than $4 million from investors. Davis falsely told investors that their money would be placed in a Five-Star Bank certificate of deposit, where it would earn as much as 13 percent interest with little risk to the investors' principal.

In reality, the Five-Star Bank CD did not exist, and Davis stole the investors' money. He was sentenced to ten years in prison and ordered to pay three point five million dollars in restitution.

When Connie made it to the conference room for her meeting, Harrison Davis was seated with another man that she had never met next to him. The two men were sitting close to each other and whispering.

"If I had known that you were bringing somebody, we could have made this a double date," she said when she came into the conference room with an armful of files.

"Ms. Lewis, this is my attorney, Theodore Austin," Davis said.

"What happened to Ms. Hawkins?" Connie asked as she put her things down.

Kinsley Hawkins had represented Davis in his wire fraud trial. She was a very pretty woman, with long, black hair, deep-set brown eyes, and the type of lips that made Angela Joliet famous. It was clear to Connie from the start that there was more than an attorney-client relationship between them, and maybe that was why she was representing him. She may have been a capable tax attorney, but Kinsley Hawkins was clearly out of her depth in his wire fraud trial.

"Mrs. Hawkins no longer represents Mr. Davis's interests in this matter," Austin said.

"I take it then that you'll be handling Mr. Davis's appeal"—she sorted through her papers—"of the ten-year sentence for wire fraud charges, correct?"

"That's correct."

"Excellent. I believe that you'll find our conversation today both interesting and beneficial to your client. First off, I want to thank you, gentlemen, for coming in this morning. I only have a few questions for your client," she said and turned on the recorder. "By your acknowledgment that I am recording this interview, you concede that any statement you make is voluntary and is not the product of coercive questioning and is not tainted by the existence of prior unwarned statements." She paused. "It's not a sworn oath. It's just something I like to do to cover myself."

"I understand completely, Ms. Lewis, and on behalf of my client, I will so concede," Austin said.

"Excellent. Let's get started." Connie took the folder from the top of her pile and opened it in front of her. "I'm interested in what your client can tell me about The Green Ridge Development Corporation."

Davis leaned close to Austin, and they began whispering. While they talked, Connie organized the folders in the order she would need based on his answers to her questions.

"That is a very broad question, Ms. Lewis. Could you be more specific?" Austin said.

"What can your client tell me about his involvement with Daniel Beason, Elias Colton, Quentin Hunter, and The Green Ridge Development Corporation?"

Davis leaned close to Austin, and the two began whispering again. Connie knew when she asked that it was too broad a question, but she wanted him to think about it before making her next move.

"That still too broad a question for you?" she paused for a moment to see if they had a response. "Let me help you out with that." Connie pulled a piece of paper from one of the files she'd arranged in front of her. "Maybe that will refresh your memory."

She handed Austin the paper. After giving them a second or two to look it over, she continued.

"You'll notice that it is a page from the audit of your bank, National Savings Life. What I'd like is for your client to explain the line item highlighted in yellow."

Davis got his glasses from his pocket, put them on, and looked at the document. He looked at Austin and then took a hard look at Connie before he leaned closed to Austin and began whispering once more. After three minutes of that, Connie started to gather her files.

"I'm going to give you gentlemen some time to discuss this." She stood up. "Take as much time as you need. Just let somebody know when you're ready, and they'll get me," Connie said on her way out of the conference room.

It was more than half an hour later when she was informed that they were ready to talk.

"So," Connie said when she came back into the conference room and sat down, "what can your client tell me about his involvement with Daniel Beason, Elias Colton, Quentin Hunter, and The Green Ridge Development Corporation?"

"Before we go any further," Austin said and cleared his throat, "you mentioned something about finding this conversation to be beneficial to my client."

Connie smiled because this was where she wanted to be. She just didn't think she'd get there so quickly. "I did."

"If you don't mind, can we talk about *that* first?"

"Mr. Austin, your client is out on bail awaiting appeal of his ten-year sentence. Today, and *only* today, I am in a position to make half of those years disappear." She was able to make him that offer because it was the same plea deal that she had offered to Kinsley Hawkins, which she rejected and opted to go to trial.

Once again, Davis leaned close to Austin, and the two began whispering. Connie had a feeling that this wouldn't be a long conversation, so she waited.

"The line item in question was made to cover an illegal $300,000 loan that Quentin Hunter pressured my client into making to Daniel Beason, who was his partner in the Green Ridge land deal along with Elias Colton," Austin said and put his hand on Davis's shoulder. "My client was the victim of powerful men who forced him to give them the loan."

And that was *precisely* what she wanted to hear. So after asking them a few more questions to get the specifics of the interaction, Connie stood up and thanked Davis and his attorney for coming. Then, after passing them off to Monique Fuller in the legal department, Connie made an appointment to speak with Quentin Hunter, CEO of Innovative Investments.

"First off, I want to thank you for taking this meeting on such short notice, Mr. Hunter."

"Not a problem. I am, however, curious to know what this is all about, Ms. Lewis," Quentin said.

"I have a few questions about your involvement with The Green Ridge Development Corporation."

Chapter Eighteen

"Thank you, Mr. Hunter. If I have any further questions, I'll be in touch," Connie said and closed the file that she had in front of her.

"You still haven't told me what this is about, Ms. Lewis," Quentin said as she stood up and put her file in her Simon Miller two-tone leather tote.

"As I said, Mr. Hunter, these are just routine questions."

"Am I under investigation?" he asked and stood up.

"No, Mr. Hunter. Currently, you are not the subject of a federal investigation," she said as she made her way to the door.

"I'm not sure I like the sound of 'currently.' That is a *very* open-ended statement, Ms. Lewis," he said as he walked out of his office with her.

Connie stopped at the door. "I assure you, Mr. Hunter, if you were the subject of a federal investigation, this interview would have gone completely differently." Connie smiled and extended her hand. "Have a nice day, Mr. Hunter."

"You too, Ms. Lewis," an angry and confused Quentin said as he watched her walk down the hall.

When she got to the elevator, Connie turned, and when she saw that he was watching, she smiled and waved before getting on the elevator, satisfied that she had accomplished her purpose. She was positive that as soon as he went back into the office, his first call would be to Daniel Beason, and Connie wanted to put something on his mind.

As she anticipated, when Quentin went back into his office, he was understandably angry because he didn't like getting blindsided by a visit from an FBI investigator. And even though she said that he wasn't the subject of a federal investigation, he was confused because he had no idea what was going on, and Connie Lewis refused to tell him the reason for her inquiry. And *that* made him angry too.

"Just routine questions" was what Connie said each time he'd ask what this interview was all about.

"'Just routine questions,' my ass," he said and got up. "That muthafucka needs to explain himself," Quentin said and left his office.

"I'm gone for the day, Samantha," he said to his personal assistant on his way out the door.

On the way to Rockville Guaranty Savings and Loan, Quentin thought about how quickly things could change. He had spent the better part of the

morning thinking about Ebony and what a lovely
evening they had.

*Would have been better if it ended with me deep
inside her, but I ain't complaining,* he chuckled.

The more time that he spent with Ebony, the
more impressed he became with her. Not only was
she beautiful and very sexy, but Ebony was also
intelligent and well on her way to achieving what
she wanted out of life. She'd told him the night
before over dinner that she was doing what she
loved to do every day. "And isn't that what life is or
should be all about?"

And she sure doesn't need an old man like you,
Quentin thought.

But then he thought about the way Ebony would
look at him sometimes.

I don't know. Maybe. You are *having dinner
with her again tonight, so perhaps she is digging
you, old man.*

He was feeling good . . . and then Connie Lewis
showed up unannounced like a cold slap in the face.
Quentin hadn't thought about The Green Ridge
Development Corporation in years, so having an
FBI investigator asking questions made him mad
as hell. Therefore, when he got to Beason's office,
he was not to be denied.

"Don't give me that 'he's in a meeting shit,'
Gwen," Quentin said as he pushed past her. "I
know he's in there."

When Quentin thrust open the door to Beason's office, Andrea Frazier quickly stood up from the end of his desk and straightened her Roland Mouret Ribbed Midi dress.

"I'm sorry, Mr. Beason," Gwen said as she followed Quentin into the office.

"It's all right, Gwen," Beason said, and Gwen closed the door.

"Could you excuse us, Andrea? I need to speak to Daniel . . . alone," Quentin added before Beason said that he could say whatever he had to say to him in front of Andrea.

"There's certainly no need for that, Quentin. I have Daniel's complete confidence."

Quentin looked at her. "Get the fuck out, Andrea."

She looked indignant, but when Beason nodded his head, Andrea looked at Quentin, and then she left the office. However, instead of closing the door behind her, she left it slightly ajar on the way out.

"Take a break, Gwen," Andrea said, and when Gwen was gone, she sat down at her desk to listen.

"What can I do for you, Quentin?" Daniel said and began straightening up the papers on his desk. "And make it quick. I have a plane to catch."

"What's going on with Green Ridge?"

Hearing the words "Green Ridge" made Beason stop what he was doing and look up at Quentin. "Nothing that I know of. Why?"

"Then tell me why an investigator, FBI Special Agent Connie Lewis, just left my office asking a shitload of questions about Green Ridge."

"What did you tell her?"

Quentin pointed in Beason's face. "That's the *wrong* answer. You were supposed to say, 'I don't know anything about it.' But you *do*, don't you?"

"No, I don't. I have no idea about any investigation into Green Ridge. But what did you tell her?"

"The truth."

"Which is?" Beason asked, and Quentin knew that something was going on, and no matter how much he denied having any knowledge of the investigation, Beason knew *exactly* what it was about.

"I told her that The Green Ridge Development Corporation was a business venture between me, you, and Elias that was incorporated to develop vacation properties but lost money."

"Anything else?"

"*Was* there anything else?" Quentin needed to know.

"No," Beason insisted, but Quentin had known him long enough to know that there was more to it.

Quentin looked at Beason for a while without speaking. "Please tell me that whatever this is, it has nothing to do with Elias getting murdered. Please tell me that."

"You're accusing me of murder?"

"No. Don't be ridiculous. You could no more kill Elias than I could. I just want to know if the two are related, that's all."

"No," Beason said emphatically. "I don't know who this Connie Lewis is or what she's investigating or what it has to do with you and Green Ridge, but I promise you, Quentin, I *will* find out." Beason stood up and put the papers into his briefcase. "But I really do have a flight to catch."

"Where are you off to now?"

"Zurich, Switzerland."

"Staying long?" Quentin asked because he needed to know when he'd be back. There was more to this, and he knew it, and he knew that whatever it was, that he needed to get out in front of it.

"Not long at all. I have a meeting in Zurich an hour after I land there, and then it's right back here after the meeting."

Quentin chuckled and started for the door. "Taking one of your usual flights with the in-flight female entertainment?"

"You know me. Always first class. Look, I'll be back the day after tomorrow, and I'll straighten out whatever is going on with . . . whatever this is. But right now—"

"I know. You have a plane to catch." Quentin started for the door, but he stopped and turned back to face Beason. "Don't fuck me on this," Quentin said with his finger in Beason's face.

"What you gonna do? Sic your gangster on me?" Quentin smiled.

"I heard about Anthony Nguyen."

Quentin had mentioned to Black that he was being held up on a deal because Anthony Nguyen hadn't signed a contract. So he told Jackie, and she sent Marvin and Baby Chris, who were able to "convince" him to sign.

"I don't know what you're talking about. Just don't fuck me on this, Daniel. That's all I'm saying."

Because, yeah, I will *sic Mike on you,* Quentin thought as he left Beason's office.

Andrea sat at Gwen's desk and watched Quentin leave. She had heard everything. When Quentin was gone, she got up and went into the office.

"What was that about?" she asked like she hadn't heard it all.

"No time. Come on. I'll explain on the way to the airport," Beason said, and he told her the story that she only knew part of.

Beason had proposed that Quentin Hunter and Elias Colton join him in buying 230 acres of undeveloped land. The goal was to subdivide the site into lots for vacation homes, hold the property for a few years, then sell the lots at a profit.

They invested $500,000 each to buy land and subsequently transferred ownership of the land to the newly created Green Ridge Development Corporation, where each had equal shares.

However, with interest rates on the rise, the real estate venture eventually failed.

When the market got better a few years later, and without Quentin's knowledge, Beason incorporated Green Ridge Estates and sold, then reacquired it through several front companies, renamed it Tree Ridge Acres, and began offering it for sale to investors.

"And between that money and the loan from Harrison Davis is how you were able to acquire Emerson," Andrea said because that's where her involvement with The Green Ridge Development Corporation began.

With the help of Donna Smith, an attorney at Powell law firm which provided legal services to Rousseau Land Development, Andrea funneled the additional one point two million dollars required by moving the money back and forth among several front companies and intermediaries. In addition to setting up the companies, Smith also helped Beason financially by providing him with consulting contracts. He never performed any actual work but was paid handsomely for it.

"What do you want me to do?"

"Reach out to any contacts you have that can tell you who this woman is and what she's investigating," he said as they arrived at the private field. The limousine pulled into the hanger of Executive Flight Lines, a business charter service, and parked in front of the Gulfstream G550. Two women in white tuxedo tails with white shirts, bow ties, and black bodysuit bottoms approached the limousines and opened his door.

"Safe trip," Andrea said as Beason got out, and the two women escorted him aboard the jet.

As the preflight instructions were being given to the other passengers, Beason was copying files from a Surface Pro tablet to a thumb drive.

"Good afternoon, gentlemen. Welcome onboard Flight 47 to Paris, France, with continuing service to Zurich, Switzerland. We are ready for takeoff and expect to be in the air in approximately seven minutes. We ask that you please fasten your seat belts at this time and secure all baggage underneath your seat or in the overhead compartments. We also ask that your seats and table trays are in the upright position for takeoff. Please turn off all personal electronic devices, including tablets and cell phones. Thank you for choosing Executive Flight Lines. And please, enjoy our hospitality during your flight," the flight attendant said.

When the instructions were concluded, an attractive woman dressed in a sexy two-piece Air Force pilot outfit with matching G-string, a little cockpit-cutie hat, and thigh-high stockings approached him.

"Would you like some company during the flight, Mr. Beason?" she asked.

"I would love some company."

She sat down next to him. "My name is Paige," she said, and Beason got lost in the depth of her cleavage as he removed the thumb drive from the tablet. Beason was distracted and briefly lost focus on the importance of the thumb drive and what it contained. Then without really paying attention to what he was doing, it fell onto the chair instead of him putting the drive into his jacket pocket.

After the seven-hour flight, Beason got off the Gulfstream in Paris. While he was off the plane, he went into the bathroom and filled the sink with water. Once it was full, he submerged the tablet under the water. When he took it out, he smashed it against the wall until it broke into pieces. Then he picked up the pieces, left the bathroom, and began dropping the broken fragments in different garbage cans on his way back to the aircraft.

As a result of bad weather, the flight arrived in Zurich an hour late, so when Beason exited the aircraft, he rushed off the plane without checking to make sure that he had the very important thumb drive that he needed for his meeting.

The flight attendant found it after the passengers exited the flight.

Chapter Nineteen

"That's it. Over there on your left," Alwan said, pointing, and Ricky parked the car outside of the building where Rain's aunt Priscilla told her that Sapphire lived.

"We're here," Alwan looked back and said to Rain.

"Yeah, I figured that out when he parked."

Instead of getting out of the car and going inside the building to do what she came there to do, Rain sat there for a while thinking about whether she truly wanted to do this. She promised her aunt that she would look into her cousin's disappearance, and Rain Robinson always kept her promise. The question was why she was doing it herself? She was the boss of The Family. Rain could have sent Alwan and Ricky to check out Sapphire's apartment and report back to her.

They're your family, Lorraine. And that counts for something. At least it should.

Rain was there because Millie said that she needed to do this. She took a minute to think

about the impact and influence that Millie always
had over her. She'd been the only constant female
presence in her life. Millie was family, more family
than her mother's family. In a way, Millie *was* her
mother, so Rain got out of the car to do what
her mother told her to do.

"I'll be back," she said and reached the handle.

"You don't want us to come with you?" Ricky
asked, and both Alwan and Rain looked at him.

"If she wanted us to come with her, she would
have said, 'Come on,' not 'I'll be back,'" Alwan said.

Rain got out laughing because Alwan was starting to sound like her.

You're a bad influence on him.

It was a nice building in a pleasant, quiet
Manhattan neighborhood, but it was nothing too
elaborate. It was about what one would expect
on a flight attendant's salary. Rain pressed the
buzzer for Sapphire's apartment, hoping that she
would be there. That would make this easy. If
Sapphire opened the door, Rain could just say,
"Hi, Sapphire, I'm your cousin, Rain. Your mama
wants you to call her."

But there was no answer.

So Rain waited near the door, pretending to be
checking her pockets until somebody came out of
the building. She quickly grabbed the door, went
inside, and caught the elevator up to Sapphire's
floor. Rain knocked on the door, and then she

tried the doorknob. She was surprised that it was unlocked. She took out her gun and slowly opened the door. Rain looked in the apartment. It had been ransacked.

"Sapphire!" Rain shouted from the doorway. But she got no answer.

She put on her gloves and stepped inside. The place was a mess. The furniture was flipped over. The couch and chair cushions were cut open, and their fillings emptied onto the floor of the one-bedroom apartment.

"Sapphire!" she shouted again as she stepped over a vase that used to have artificial flowers in it. But once more, Rain got no answer.

She moved farther into the space and could see that the kitchen was in the same condition as the rest of the place. The cabinets were opened, and the contents were thrown onto the floor. Even the refrigerator door was open, and most of the food was now on the floor.

Rain came out of the kitchen and was about to go into the bedroom when she saw something shiny on the floor that caught her attention. As she was bending over to pick it up, someone hit her in the back of the head. Rain stumbled forward, but once she caught her balance, she back kicked or Dwi Chagi her attacker in the stomach.

Another effect of her avoidance of Carter was that Rain hadn't had sex since their threesome with Miranda. Therefore, she had a lot of pent-up sexual energy and had no preferred outlet for her to release it. Consequently, she'd been working out like mad, and that included her training in Beom Seogi Taekwondo, a Korean defensive martial arts fighting style that she learned from Nick.

Her ambusher stumbled back, but he quickly regained his balance. He came at her fast and knocked her gun out of her hand. He punched her twice in the face and then tried to grab her. She responded with Meereo Chagi, a push kick to his chest. Rain repeated that same kick twice more, a technique known as Geodeup-Chagi, and her attacker went down.

As she came at him, he reached for his gun and opened fire. Rain dove for the floor as he continued firing, and she crawled behind the couch for cover. Rain pulled out her second weapon, put one in the chamber, and came up firing. Her attacker returned Rain's fire, and she dropped again for cover.

She crawled to the edge of the couch, and when he stopped firing to reload, she shot back and quickly dropped for cover. He slammed in the clip, stood up, began walking toward her, and kept firing until his gun was empty.

Rain smiled, stood up, raised her weapon, and pulled the trigger—but her gun was empty too. So she threw it at him; it missed. But it was enough of a distraction for her to step up on the couch, jump off, and connect with a crescent kick to his face, a kick known as Bandal-Chagi. It forced him back against the wall, and Rain roundhouse kicked him because Dollyo Chagi was her favorite kick.

"Fuck all this kung fu shit," he said with an accent that she didn't recognize.

He grabbed Rain before she could kick him again, picked her up, and threw her on the coffee table. It broke on impact, and he ran out of the apartment.

Even though that shit hurt like a muthafucka, Rain struggled to get to her feet and ran out into the hallway after him, but he was nowhere in sight. She went back into the apartment, collected her weapons, and got out of there, wiping the doorknob as she closed the door.

On the way to the elevator, Rain took out her phone and called Alwan.

"What's up?"

"If you see a white man in a black jumpsuit come running out of here looking like he been in a fight, stop him," she ordered, but when she got outside, her men reported that nobody had come out the front door since she called.

"Fuck," Rain shouted and got in the car.

Chapter Twenty

"You all right?" Alwan asked as Ricky drove away from the building.

"No. Take me to Perry's," Rain said, squirming in her seat because her back hurt. Then she thought about it. "No. I don't feel like hearing that nigga's mouth. Call Daniella Ramsey and ask her if she could come to my house. Don't tell her why. Just ask her to come."

"On it," Alwan said, pulling out his phone and making the call.

Ricky drove Rain to her house, and she went straight to bed thinking about her reason for being involved in this. *Because they are your family, Lorraine*, she could hear Millie saying. But whatever her reasoning was didn't matter—not anymore, Rain was in it now.

It was an hour later when Daniella Ramsey arrived at the house to treat her. Her injuries were minor. She had a busted lip and a nasty gash on her left cheek, but Rain appeared fine other than her back hurting.

"You need to come to the office so I can do a more thorough examination," Daniella said as she tended to Rain's wounds. "But let me ask you a question."

"What's that?"

"You do remember me telling you that you were pregnant a couple of days ago, right?"

Rain smiled. "I remember."

But Daniella wasn't smiling. "What part of that said you should go out and get in a fight?"

"Believe me, it wasn't my idea," she protested. But Rain was thinking about what she had gotten herself involved in, and more to the point, what Sapphire was involved in for somebody to be searching her apartment and be willing to kill her to get whatever it was. It made Rain wonder if he had found what he was looking for, which was why he ran out of there. She couldn't be sure.

"I'll give you something for the pain, but I need to see you tomorrow, Rain," Daniella said and gave her 650 mg extended-release Acetaminophen. "I'll call you later and let you know what time to come for an X-ray and tests. In the meantime, get some rest. That's an order."

"Okay."

"I'm serious, Rain. You need to stay in this bed and get some rest. And I need to see you tomorrow." She paused. "Regardless of whether you plan on having that baby, you still need to take care of yourself. And that means that I need to make sure you're all right."

"I'll see you tomorrow. You have my word," Rain said, and Daniella left the house. She was about to take the pain meds when her phone rang. "Carter" popped up on the phone screen. She shook her head. "Another nigga's mouth I don't want to hear," she said, but it might be about business, so she answered just before it when to voicemail. "This Rain."

"Where are you?"

"Why? What's up?"

"I need to talk to you, that's why."

Fuck. "Where you at?"

"On my way to J.R.'s."

"I'll meet you there," Rain said and ended the call. "Fuck," she said aloud and slowly got out of bed.

She thought about what Daniella said about her needing to rest. She was pregnant, and on top of that, she'd just had a fight, but she was the boss of The Family, so she was going. Once she was dressed, Rain put on her vest, holstered her guns, and came out of her room.

"Get the car, Ricky," Rain commanded, and he bounced up from the couch and rushed out of the room, but Alwan didn't move. Before she left, Daniella had given him specific instructions.

"Where do you think you're going?" Alwan stood up to ask.

Rain looked at him. "Excuse me?"

"I was just asking where you were going," he said in a more respectful tone. "Daniella Ramsey told me that you would be fine, but you needed to rest."

"We're going to J.R.'s. I need to talk to Carter. Now, come on," Rain said and walked past him, but he still didn't move.

"Why can't Carter come here? Daniella Ramsey told me that you needed to rest, Rain," he said pleadingly.

Realizing that his out-of-character defiance was out of concern for her, Rain walked back to him. "I appreciate you looking out for me, but I'm fine, Alwan, really."

"You sure?"

"I'm sure," she said reassuringly and put her hand on his shoulder. "I'm fine. And when I'm not, I promise I'll let you know."

"Okay."

"Now, let's go get this over with, so I can come back here and take my ass to bed," she said and started walking. "My back hurts like a mutha-fucka."

"I thought you said you were fine?" he asked and followed Rain to the door.

"I'm okay enough to ride to J.R.'s and talk to Carter," Rain said on her way out of the house.

Ricky opened the door for her, and once Alwan told him that they were going to J.R.'s, he started the car and headed in that direction.

"And take your time. She don't need a whole lot of bumps," Alwan said. Rain settled into her seat, glad that Alwan was her bodyguard.

Since it was still early in the evening, the club wasn't open yet. The only staff there were those who were preparing the club to open for the evening. Therefore, Rain was surprised to see that Chelsea was there.

"What happened to your face?" she asked as Rain approached her.

"What are you doing here?" she asked instead of answering.

"I asked Demi if I could come in early so she can show me the opening procedures," she said, and then Chelsea quickly added, "I'm not on the clock. I'm doing this on my own time."

"Go clock in. Nobody works for me for free," Rain said and continued to her office. She was surprised when she opened the door to her office and saw Carter sitting on the couch.

"What the fuck happened to your face?"

Rain walked past him, unholstering her guns. "I had a fight," she said and sat down at her desk.

"With whom?" he demanded to know. She told him about Sapphire and what happened when she went to her apartment.

"Why didn't you call me?" Carter asked, and Rain said nothing. He shook his head because Rain was frustrating. "You shouldn't have gone there alone."

"I wasn't alone. Alwan and Ricky were with me."

"Were they outside?" he asked because Rain always told them to wait outside.

"Yes."

"Then you were alone." He shook his head. "You're pregnant, Rain. You shouldn't be out there fighting." Carter got up to refill his drink.

"I wasn't planning on getting in a fight." Rain smiled. "You know I'd rather shoot a nigga than kick his ass."

"You should have told me about this." Carter shot his drink and poured another. "I should have been there with you."

Although he told Rain that he wasn't ready to be a father since she said she was thinking about having it, Carter had been rethinking it, and he was slowly warming to the idea. He went and sat in front of Rain's desk.

"I can take care of myself. You know that."

"I know you can. You're Rain Robinson. You're a *bad* bitch. That's what everybody tells me. But you are *not* indestructible, Rain."

"At least I didn't get shot this time," Rain laughed, but Carter saw no humor in it at all.

"This ain't no joke. You're pregnant, and you need to let me handle this," he said, and Rain stood up.

"Okay."

"What?"

"You want to handle it, handle it." She holstered her guns and came from behind her desk. "Why don't you grab Geno and them and roll by her apartment—see what you can find out."

"Where are you going?"

"Home to bed," she said and walked past him because he was starting to get on her nerves. "Call me later and let me know what you find out."

She walked out of her office. "Let's go," she said, and Alwan and Ricky stood up and followed her downstairs.

"Alwan," Carter said, and he came back to him. "Don't let her out of your sight, you hear me?"

"Yeah, Carter, I hear you. But you need to tell *her* that because you know she don't listen to me," he said and went down the stairs to catch up.

"She don't listen to me either."

On the way back to Rain's house, she got a call back from Vonetta Jernigan, a friend of Sapphire's. Aunt Priscilla had reached out to her when Sapphire first disappeared. Rain had called and had left a message for her to call if she heard from her. After a bit of resistance from Alwan, who repeated what Daniella Ramsey told him about her needing to rest, Rain told Ricky to take them there.

"It's on the way," Rain said to appease him, even though it wasn't. "And then we go straight home."

"Okay," Alwan said reluctantly, and Ricky drove on.

When they got to Vonetta's Upper Eastside apartment building and parked the car, both Alwan and Ricky looked in the backseat at Rain. She smiled. "Let's go," she said, and they got out of the car.

When they got to the apartment, Alwan knocked on the door.

"Who is it?"

"Rain Robinson."

"Just a minute," Vonetta said. Moments later, she opened the door dressed in a La Perla Exotique silk halter lace-trim nightdress and robe.

"Wait here," Rain said, and both men looked at her.

"Carter said not to let you out of my sight," Alwan whispered, but his eyes were glued on Vonetta because she had nothing on under that lace-trim nightdress, and he could see straight through it.

"Okay. Ricky, you wait out here. Alwan, you're with me," Rain said, and Alwan happily followed her into Vonetta's laid apartment.

"Thank you for coming right away," Vonetta said as she led Rain into the living room. "I'm expecting a guest soon, but I've been so worried about Fire since her mother called me."

"Fire?" Rain questioned.

Vonetta giggled. "That's what she likes to be called. She gets mad if you call her Sapphire."

Sound like anybody you know? Rain thought.

She hated being called Lorraine. To her, it was like chalk scratching across a blackboard every time. The only one that she tolerated it from was Millie and now Aunt Priscilla, but it had the same effect on her.

"I know what that's like, believe me."

"Anyway, I haven't heard from Fire in a while, and I wanted to help."

"You think something might have happened to her? I mean, does she hang around with the kind of people that something *would* happen to her?"

"Fire gets around, so it's possible."

"Can you think of anybody that might be looking for her? Trying to find something?"

"Not that I can think of," she sighed. "Truth is, we're not as close as we used to be when we worked for the same escort agency. We still talk, but it's not the same, you know what I mean? But we haven't seen each other in months, so I can't really say for sure."

"So, Fire's an escort?"

"I'm sorry. I thought you knew."

"I thought that she was a flight attendant," Rain said because that's what her aunt told her. "So you don't know anything about her working at a place called Overseas Air, do you?"

Vonetta thought for a second or two. "I've heard of them. Fire mentioned them once, but I don't know much about them except Fire said the people involved are bad news, and I should stay away from them."

"Can you think of anybody else I can talk to that might know something?"

"No, sorry, I don't. I'm not much help, am I?"

Rain stood up. "No, you've been a big help," she said because Vonetta had been a big help. But now that Rain knew that she was an escort and not a flight attendant, it changed things. She started for the door. "If you think of anything or you hear from Fire, please, call me."

"I will," Vonetta said, and Alwan opened the door for Rain.

"Thanks," Rain said and left the apartment. "Take me home. All this walking is making my back hurt."

Chapter Twenty-one

When they got to Rain's house, Alwan and Ricky made themselves comfortable. She was tired, and her back hurt, so Rain didn't even bother to give them a hard time about why they were setting up camp in her living room. She just went up to bed.

"Good night."

"Good night, Rain," Alwan said and watched her move slowly up the stairs as Ricky turned on the television.

Rain got undressed and took a hot shower. When she had dried off, she got in bed, but she was unable to sleep. There was too much on her mind for that. Naturally, the fact that she was pregnant topped the list. She still hadn't decided whether she was going to have it. Rain thought about her life and what kind of mother she'd be. She feared that any child of hers would grow up to be just like her, and *that* weighed heavily on her mind. She was a killer. A "murdering psychopath" was what some called her. Rain laughed every time she heard it, so maybe motherhood wasn't for her.

But now she was more concerned about what her cousin, Sapphire, *excuse me, Fire,* Rain giggled, was involved in. So she tossed and turned but was unable to fall asleep. She had just drifted off to sleep when she was startled by a knock at her door.

"What?" she shouted, and the door opened. "Carter? Fuck you doing here?"

"Damn. Really?" Carter asked. He came there because he was concerned about her, and this was the response he got. *That hurt.* "I came to make sure you're all right."

"I'm fine," Rain said and rolled over, hoping that he would take the hint that she didn't want to be bothered with him and leave. *Fuck.* "You go by Fire's apartment?" she asked since he was just standing there.

"Me and Geno went by there."

Carter was horrified when he saw how much damage there was in the apartment and wondered if it was all the result of the fight. Rain was pregnant, and she was pregnant with *his* child. Carter felt terrible for not being there with her, but what could he do? Once Rain made up her mind to do something, there was no turning her around, and she had made it obvious to him that she was done with him. He was good with that, but she was pregnant with *his* child, which changed everything for Carter. Although he was getting used to the idea, he wasn't ready to be a father. He was, by no means, a perfect man. Some, namely Mileena, might say that he wasn't even a *good* man, so his fear, like Rain's, was he could ruin his baby's life by not being a perfect father.

"We didn't find anything."

"Cops been there?"

"I don't think so. I mean, there was no crime scene tape on the door," he said. More silence filled the room as Carter waited on Rain to say something, and she waited for him to leave. She turned over, and they looked stone-faced at each other until Carter finally said, "Don't you think you need to talk to me?"

"About what?" she asked as her phone rang, knowing that he was right. They *did* need to talk, but she wasn't ready to have that conversation with him yet—mostly because she didn't know what she was going to do.

"About you being pregnant," *with my child,* he thought but didn't say aloud as Rain answered her phone.

"This Rain."

"It's Carla." After Rain talked to her aunt Priscilla, she reached out to Carla to see if she could track Fire down and find out whatever information she could about Overseas Air. "I'm sorry it took me so long, but I finally found something on Overseas Air."

Rain sat up in bed. "What you got for me, Carla?"

"They don't have much of an online footprint, so I couldn't find out much about them. All I was able to get was an address."

"Send it to my phone." She looked at Carter and got out of bed. Since he wasn't going anywhere, and she couldn't sleep, they might as well check it out.

"Done," Carla said.

Rain glanced at her phone. "Got it."

"If I find out anything else, I'll call you."

"Thanks, Carla," Rain said and ended the call.

"Where are you going?" Carter asked.

"Carla got an address for Overseas Air."

"And?"

"We're gonna check it out," she said and started getting dressed.

"No." Carter shook his head, and Rain rolled her eyes at him. "Give *me* the address, and *I'll* check it out. You need to rest."

"You're right. I do need to rest . . . but I'm going." She put on her vest. "So if you wanna come with me, fine. If not, take your ass home, and I'll handle it myself."

"I'm coming with you."

"Good. Now shut up and let's go," she said and left her bedroom, holstering her guns as she walked.

Knowing that she was in no mood for conversation, Carter said nothing on the way to Overseas

Air. But as he drove, it was all that he could think about. At times, Carter thought that having a baby would be kinda cool. They could do all the fun stuff he didn't do with his father and be the incredible father that his wasn't. But then he'd think about any time he was around babies. Crying, shitty diapers, and his lack of interest made Carter wonder if having one of his own at this point in his life would make him lose his mind.

When they got to the private airfield where Carla told her that Overseas Air was located, they drove past the other hangers until they got to the one they were looking for. It was a dump. The Overseas Air sign was rusted out, and the letters were faded. The hanger itself was in desperate need of a fresh coat of paint. Carter parked in front, and they got out of the car.

"This is the place," he said, looking up at the sign as he and Rain walked toward the building.

"If Fire's an escort, what would she have to do with an outfit like this?" Rain asked, and it made her think of something else that bothered her. If she *was* an escort like Vonetta said, Fire certainly wasn't living lavish and stylish like her friend. That could just mean that Vonetta was better at her job than Fire. But Rain had a feeling that it was something else.

When they entered the hanger, they saw four small aircraft and four men working in them. Their entrance into the hanger caused the men inside to stop what they were doing as they approached.

"Can I help you?" one of them said with a heavy European accent—the same accent that Rain had heard earlier at Sapphire's apartment.

"I'm looking for Sapphire Langston. She goes by the name Fire. Is she here?" Rain asked as more men seemed to appear out of nowhere.

"Never heard of her," one said as two more men came and stood next to him.

"I was told that she worked here," Rain said, and now they were surrounded by five men, some of whom were armed.

"And I said that I never heard of no Fire," he laughed. "Now, you need to get out before we carry you out."

Carter laughed. "Not happening," he said, shaking his head. "I mean, you can try, but it won't go well for you."

Rain looked at him. Awhile ago, he was fussing at her about putting herself in dangerous situations while pregnant, and here he was, trying to escalate the situation.

She started backing up because they were seriously outnumbered *and* outgunned. They said that they'd never heard of her. That and Fire telling Vonetta that the people involved were bad news was good enough for her.

"Fuck you, nigger," another said, raised his weapon, and began firing at Rain and Carter.

They returned fire and ran toward the hanger entrance. Unfortunately, there weren't many places to take cover in the wide-open space as the men broke out heavier weapons and sprayed the area with bullets.

They separated. Rain dove for the ground, and Carter ran for cover behind a plane. She crawled along the floor to make it to a spot where she could get to her feet and get in the firefight. Carter fired a couple of shots as he moved to the entrance. As the men continued firing at him, Rain moved toward the hanger door, firing shots as she ran. She made it to cover behind some fifty-gallon drums and began firing . . . until she smelled gas.

"Oh shit," she said when she realized that gasoline was in those drums. She started to move to a better spot, but then she had an idea.

Rain kicked over each of the drums, and as the gas spilled out onto the floor, she fired both of her guns until the gas ignited and burst into flames. When the men saw the fire spread quickly throughout the hanger, they turned their attention to getting fire extinguishers to control the blaze. Then with their focus on the fire, Rain and Carter made a run for the door and got outta there.

Chapter Twenty-two

The following morning at the offices of Pearson MDS General Contracting, Ebony was working on the articles of incorporation for the new consulting company that Marvin wanted to start when Kaloni knocked on the door. Ebony waved her in.

"What's up?"

"Sorry to bother you, Ebony, but Sataria is on the phone for you."

"For *me?*" Ebony questioned. "Is Marvin here?"

"He is."

"And she wants to talk to *me?*"

"She asked for you."

"Put her through."

"Okay, but before I do that, I need to tell you that something is going on between them, and maybe you don't want to get in the middle of it."

"Why? What's going on?"

Kaloni looked around, stepped into Ebony's office, and closed the door. "I don't know what's going on exactly," she said in a hushed tone, "but Marvin told me that he did *not* want to talk to her.

He said that I should tell her that he is not in the office and he hasn't been here if she calls."

"When was this?"

"The day that she came up here," Kaloni said. "What do you want me to do?"

"Tell her that I'll call her back," Ebony said and stood up. She was going to talk to Marvin, but then she thought about it. Even though she and Marvin were partners, to maintain their double minority status, Sataria was the majority owner. Therefore, technically, Ebony worked for Sataria, so she needed to tread lightly until she got more information. "No, wait a minute before you do that," she said and picked up her phone.

Not knowing what it was about and not wanting Sataria to think that she was avoiding her as well, Ebony sent a text that said that she was in a meeting and that she would call her back and then waited for a response. Once Sataria responded, okay, Ebony told Kaloni to go ahead and give Sataria the message while she went to talk to Marvin.

He was on the phone talking to one of the contractors about the community center when Ebony tapped on his door. He waved her in. She entered and sat down. Marvin seemed like he was in a much better mood than the night when she left him in the office to have dinner with Quentin. He said he had a lot on his mind, and they would talk about it the following morning, but it had slipped her mind.

That's because you were way too giddy about your date with Quentin, Ebony thought as Marvin began wrapping up his call. She had to admit that he was the most interesting man she'd been out with in a very long time. And the fact that he was a mature man and seemingly not into the mind games like so many younger men she'd dated made him that much more appealing.

And the whole bald head and that salt-and-pepper goatee are very sexy, she thought, so she was looking forward to having dinner with him again that night.

"Morning, Ebony," Marvin said when he hung up.

She was right. He was in a good mood that morning, much better than he had been the previous days. After finalizing the Spring Hill Media Group contracts with Savannah Russell, Marvin had a drink with Savannah to celebrate, several to be exact. The evening ended with them sharing a kiss that said, *"Not this time, but I will have you next time."* And when he got back to the hotel, Joslin was waiting for him in the lobby.

"Good morning, Marvin." She paused and took a breath. "Is there something going on between you and Sataria that I need to know about?"

"Yes, there is," he said and got up. "Let's take a walk."

Ebony got up and followed him out of his office.

"We'll be right back, Kaloni," he said as they passed her desk and walked out of the building. "I need you to dissolve the company," he said once they had walked for a while.

"What company?"

"This one. Pearson MDS."

"*What?*" Ebony asked because she couldn't believe what she was hearing. She and Marvin had worked hard to merge the two companies after Serek died. His wanting to dissolve it made no sense.

"I don't care how much it costs, but I need you to do whatever you have to do to separate Sataria from the company."

This is why Sataria wanted to talk to me, Ebony thought. Kaloni was right. She didn't want to get in the middle of whatever was going on between them, but there she was, about to dive right in.

"Okay, Marvin. As your friend *and* your lawyer, I'm going to need you to tell me what is going on."

Now, it was Marvin who took a deep breath. "I'm done with Sataria," he said and told Ebony that after Serek beat Sataria, he killed him.

"I knew that."

"Yeah, but what you *don't* know is that Serek wasn't her first husband, and I'm not the first man that she got to kill for her," Marvin said to a shocked Ebony. He went on to tell her about being approached by her cousin's husband, Cleavon, and listening to the recording of Sataria bragging that she could get him to do anything for her. And then Marvin opened up to Ebony and told her how much it hurt him that she would use him like that.

"And I loved her, Ebony." He paused. "I never really loved anybody before," Marvin chuckled, "I didn't even know what love was until I loved her." *How could she have done that to us?*

"I'm sorry, Marvin," Ebony said empathetically.

"But she was right about me. I was just that weak for her. I would have done anything for her—and I did. I did *exactly* what she wanted."

Ebony stopped walking. "Did you tell her that you killed Serek?" she asked because the time for the empathetic friend was over. Now it was time for the lawyer in her to come out.

"No. I told her that I had nothing to do with it, and she never brought it up after that," Marvin said, thinking that should have told him something.

"Good," his now-angry lawyer said. "Don't worry anymore about that business. Just do what you have to do to heal, and I'll take care of Sataria for you."

"Thanks, Ebony."

"You think she'll be willing to be bought out?"

"I'm sure of it. Sataria has no interest in running a construction company." Serek had taken out a $10 million insurance policy with a double indemnity clause on each of them. Therefore, his murder netted Sataria $20 million. "She'll take the money," Marvin said, thinking that she had men killed for money.

She'd do anything for money.

"I'll get on that right away."

"The sooner I'm done with her, the better I'll feel," he said. They started back to the office when Ebony stopped again.

"I can buy Sataria out, no problem, but it's going to mess up our double minority status. We have current and future contracts that are tied to that status," she warned.

"I didn't think about that," Marvin said and thought about what to do. "How about this? After buying her out, we sell the company to the new consulting company that we're forming. Then change the ownership percentage from each of us having equal shares to you and Dominica owning 26 percent. That would make you two majority owners, and we keep our double minority status. What do you think?"

Ebony thought about it. "That could work," she said, and that would take care of the business end of it, but she was still worried about Marvin.

Chapter Twenty-three

That evening, Quentin and Ebony had dinner at Ai Fiori, which showcased modern interpretations of traditional dishes from the Italian and French Riviera. It was located in the stylish Langham Hotel on Fifth Avenue. Because each had a lot on their minds, they dined quietly on Ippoglosso, Atlantic halibut, in a Livornese sauce, and Anatra, pan-roasted breast of duck.

Quentin was thinking about what could be going on with Daniel Beason and Green Ridge that an FBI investigator would come and question him about it. Although Beason said that he knew nothing about it, Quentin had known him long enough to know that Beason wasn't opposed to doing things that weren't entirely legitimate. He had come to Quentin once and asked if he wanted to invest in a new shipping venture with him. Beason promised that he would be able to more than quadruple his money within a year. When Quentin asked what they would be shipping, Beason answered, "It's best not to ask. *Just know that your money is guaranteed.*" Quentin walked away.

It was the reason that he stopped doing business with him. But they were friends, good friends, and had been since their college years. That friendship meant something to him, and all he could do was hope that it still meant something to Beason for him to be honest enough to tell him what was going on when he got back from Zurich.

Ebony's mind was on Marvin.

After her conversation with Marvin, she called Dominica into her office and told her that she needed a valuation of the company done right away. Dominica quickly delegated that job to Kandy and Melicia, and then she came right back to Ebony's office.

"What is going on?"

She was on the phone with Kaloni when Sataria called. She thought something was up when she saw Kaloni go into Ebony's office. Then Marvin and Ebony went for a walk, and when they came back, suddenly, a valuation of the company was needed immediately.

"Give it up."

Without going into the what and why, Ebony told Dominica they were buying Sataria out and reorganizing under the new consulting company, which was all she needed to know. As far as Dominica was concerned, she worked for an enterprising young man who owned a construction company and a few other businesses and knew nothing of The Family and its involvement. They spent the rest of the day working on it, but Ebony's mind was on Marvin. She wanted to do something to help ease his pain . . . more than just take Sataria off his neck, but it was a start.

After dinner, Quentin drove Ebony to her house. She hadn't said too much over dinner, and he was curious if he had said the wrong thing. Was he moving too fast, or was he going too slow? Did Ebony decide that she wasn't interested in dating an older man somewhere between cocktails and their meal? He needed to know, so he asked.

"Penny for your thoughts," Quentin said as he drove her home. She had been staring out the window, and although he enjoyed looking at her profile because he thought Ebony was breathtaking, he wondered what she was thinking about.

"Excuse me?"

He chuckled. "It's an old expression," he said, afraid that he had shown his age. "It's what people used to say when someone looks sad, or they haven't said very much for a while."

"I know what it means," Ebony giggled. "I'm not *that* young. I just didn't hear what you said."

He laughed. "I don't know which is worse . . . feeling embarrassed or feeling old."

"You're not old." She smiled and patted his thigh. "You're what they used to call 'seasoned.'"

"A polite way of saying old."

"And the same could be said for you," Ebony said instead of saying, *You may be older than me, but you are very sexy.* "You haven't had much to say tonight either."

"True. I do have a lot on my mind." He paused. "No, that's not true. I have *one* thing in particular on my mind," Quentin said as he parked in front of Ebony's house. "So, I apologize if I haven't been good company tonight."

"No apology needed. Is it anything you want to talk about?"

"You know what? You're a lawyer," Quentin smiled. "One of the most versatile and best legal minds in the organization, according to Mike Black. And since he's not known for throwing around compliments unless they are aimed squarely at his wife, I'd say that's pretty high praise."

"You know that I was shocked to hear him say that."

"As he said, you're being modest."

"Tell you what . . . Why don't you come in? I'll make us a drink, and you can tell me what's going on with you."

Quentin smiled because he was trying to think of a way to invite himself in, and she had just saved him the trouble. "Sounds good," he said and got out to open Ebony's door for her. Then he followed her to the house thinking, *Yeah, I'm fuckin' you tonight.*

Ebony and Quentin went into her house, and while he made himself comfortable in the living room, she went and changed into something more leisurely. She emerged wearing a scoop neck and sleeveless, tie-dye drawstring fitted jumpsuit with a black hazy twist design. Quentin watched hungrily as Ebony made them drinks, thinking, *Yeah, I'm* definitely *fuckin' you tonight*.

Once she handed Quentin his drink, she sat close to him on the couch, and he told her the story of The Green Ridge Development Corporation and about the visit he had from Connie Lewis.

"The plan was to hold the property for a few years and then sell the lots at a profit."

"What happened?"

"We put up five hundred thousand each to buy 230 acres of undeveloped land, and the ownership was transferred to The Green Ridge Development Corporation. We all had equal shares."

"So, what did Connie Lewis want with you?"

He told her that she had been looking into the failure of Emerson Savings & Loan and the sale to Beason, found connections between Rockville Guaranty Savings and Loan and The Green Ridge Development Corporation. "And she was interested in Davis and an insurance company called National Savings Life."

When he finished, Ebony took his glass and got up to make them another drink.

"Thank you," he said when she handed him the glass. "By the time the Green Ridge lots were surveyed and available for sale, interest rates had climbed nearly 20 percent."

Ebony sat down. "Not an attractive market for prospective buyers looking to purchase a vacation home."

"Rather than take a loss on the venture, we decided to build a model home and wait for better economic conditions."

"That's it?"

"As far as I knew, other than Daniel asking me for additional money that he said was for interest payments on the loan and other expenses. I thought the business was dead. I had written it off years ago."

"You sound like you didn't believe him."

"To tell you the truth, at that point, I really didn't care. We had a little falling out over another business matter, so it was easier just to write him out a check to get rid of him."

"Apparently, that didn't last long."

"Friendship is stronger than money," he said, looking at Ebony's full and kissable-looking lips while admiring the way her hair drifted in front of her dark eyes.

"For some," she said, staring into his eyes, not knowing how true that was in Beason's case.

Quentin had no knowledge that Beason used those additional funds plus money that he got from leveraging the Green Ridge lots to acquire the Emerson Savings and Loan, which he renamed Rockville Guaranty Savings and Loan.

"You're beautiful," Quentin said, leaning closer to Ebony.

"Thank you," she said, moving closer to him, and their lips met in a very slow and passionate kiss.

His hands began to explore her body. He felt her braless nipple through her tie-dye top. Quentin eased the strap off her shoulder and sucked her nipple. She held his head in place as he pulled down the other strap and began lightly squeezing her other nipple between his thumb and forefinger. Ebony moaned, and her legs opened wide.

Quentin knew that he had to taste her.

As he was enjoying the feeling of her nipple in his mouth, Quentin eased off the couch and settled into the perfect position to ease his tongue inside her. Ebony pulled the top over her head as Quentin kissed his way down to her navel, slowly pulling her pants down. She wasn't wearing any panties. *I guess she was expecting me,* he thought, reaching between her legs to finger her clit.

Quentin touched her thighs with both of his hands, sliding his hands up and down while he looked up into her eyes.

"You're so beautiful, Ebony," he said, then slid his tongue inside her and sucked her moist lips gently. Her clit grew harder as he licked her with the tip of his tongue, and her body began to quiver.

Ebony moaned as he very deliberately spread her lips with his thumb and forefinger while making small circles around her clit. He slid his tongue inside her and then sucked her moist lips gently. She felt her body quiver as he licked her clit with the tip of his tongue.

When he felt her body jerk, he started nibbling on her clit, and her juices began flowing down his chin. Quentin sucked up all her sweet juices, and Ebony's thighs pressed together. She flinched, and her thighs tightened around his head before her body convulsed uncontrollably.

Quentin stood up quickly, took off his shirt, pulled down his pants, got back down on his knees, and entered her slowly. He leaned forward, caressing and then sucking her bouncing breasts. Ebony was tossing it right back at him as he thrust himself into her again and again, and each time, it felt like he was going deeper than before.

When he felt her walls tighten around him, he thrust his hips into her with enough intensity that she screamed, "Oh shit," as she came.

Ebony pushed him off her and got up on her knees. Quentin stood up, kicked off his shoes, and stepped out of his pants. He stroked his erection and got behind her. Then he grabbed her hips and entered her. She was so wet, and he was so hard for her that he began to pump it in her as hard as he could.

He reached for her shoulders and pounded into her. The feeling of her spasming around him felt so amazing to him that he felt himself about to come. Ebony felt it too, and she gyrated her hips and took it from him.

"Oh shit," he yelled as he came.

Chapter Twenty-four

For Quentin, it had been a beautiful morning because he had Ebony on his mind. The
morning after they made love, he took her to
the Morning Star Café for breakfast. And then,
even though it was the weekend, she went to work.
She wanted to continue working on buying Sataria
out of Pearson MDS Construction. As for Quentin,
he was on his way home, feeling amazing, when he
stopped at a red light.

While he waited for the light to change, his
mind slowly turned from thoughts of Ebony's lus-
cious body to thoughts of Daniel Beason, Connie
Lewis, and the investigation into The Green Ridge
Development Corporation. He barely remembered
Harrison Davis or him having any involvement
in Green Ridge. Connie Lewis had to refresh his
memory before he recalled the meeting. He remembered that Beason called and said that he was
tied up with something. Quentin couldn't remem-

ber what exactly and asked him if he could meet with Davis. He said that Davis had agreed to loan him $300,000 for the project, but he never threatened him.

Quentin wanted desperately to give Beason the benefit of the doubt and believe that he knew nothing about it. "But you know better . . . don't you?" he questioned aloud as the light changed.

Regardless of whether Beason was telling the truth, Connie Lewis wasn't just asking general questions about Green Ridge. All of her questions were explicitly about Daniel Beason's involvement in The Green Ridge Development Corporation. There was an investigation going on, and investigators love to follow the money.

And if that were the case, "And it is," Quentin knew that there was somebody that he needed to call.

"Morning, Quentin," Black said when he answered.

"Morning, Mike. I didn't wake you, did I?"

"No. I get up when my boys get up. It's only Cassandra and Michelle that get to sleep late around here these days."

That morning, Black was in the media room with his sons. Easy was sitting on the floor playing *Final Fantasy* on his PlayStation console, and

Mansa was trying to walk and doing more falling than walking.

"I know it's early, but there's something that I need to talk to you about."

"What's up?"

"It's not something that I want to talk about over the phone."

"Sound serious."

"It could be. You mind if I come out?"

"Come through. I'm not going anywhere," Black said and ended the call as Michelle came dragging into the room and sat down in the chair next to her father.

"Morning, Daddy."

"Morning, sleepyhead." Black smiled at her and put the phone down. "I'm glad you're up. Mr. Hunter is coming out to talk, and I need you to watch your brothers for me."

"I don't need anybody to watch me," Easy said without losing focus on the confrontation at the top of Shinra headquarters.

"Watch your brother," Black corrected.

"No worries, I'm not going anywhere. Y'all took my keys, remember?"

"Your *mother* took your keys. I just supported her decision. But do you understand *why* she took them?"

Because she is personally in charge of ruin-ing my life and making sure I have no fun, she thought. "Because I came home at two in the morning."

"That's part of it, but you lied to her, and you know I'm not having that. You knew when you rolled out of here that you weren't gonna be back by ten." Black smiled. "And I didn't even tell her about the clothes."

"Clothes?"

Black looked at her. "You left in one outfit and came back in another." Michelle smiled. "What? You think I didn't notice that?"

"I was hoping, but I should have known better. You never miss anything."

"So don't try to get away with anything," Black said and thought about what Shy said.

I know all her little tricks.

"Anyway, watch your brother for me until your mother gets up."

"Yes, Daddy." She looked around the room. "Where is the little rug rat?"

"He's right over—" he turned and pointed. "He was over there a second ago," Black said, and he and Michelle sprang to their feet and rushed out of the room. Easy, of course, didn't move. Shinra's son Rufus assumed control of the company and fought Cloud, so he wasn't moving from that spot.

"He wasn't in there when I came in," Michelle said as they looked in the area outside of the study.

"He couldn't have gotten far," Black said as they got to the living room in time to see that Mansa had made his way up on the couch and was reaching for the lamp.

"Oh no, you don't," Joanne said and grabbed him just before he reached it.

When Joanne developed a persistent cough that turned into difficulty breathing and then developed a pain in her back that was worsening by the day, she called Dr. Mensforth, her oncologist, and scheduled a follow-up examination to check for any symptoms or signs of cancer recurrence. Despite everything that went on between him and Shy and Black threatening to kill him, he did save Bobby's life. And besides, Dr. Spencer Mensforth was one of the top oncologists in the city; therefore, he was still her oncologist.

Joanne picked Mansa up and carried him away from the lamp. "No, no, young man. No touch."

"Thank you, Joanne," Black said.

Michelle rushed up to her. "I got him, Grandma." She took Mansa from her grandmother.

"Thank you, Michelle. That boy is getting so heavy," she said and sat down, fanning herself.

"Come on, rug rat," Michelle said, carrying him away as he reached for the lamp as he passed.

"Let's go jump on the bed and wake up Mommy. Won't that be fun?"

Joanne looked at Black. "Now, you and I both know that Sandy is *not* going to like that." She shook her head. "I don't know why Michelle chooses to torment her mother," she laughed. "Yes, I do. She's just rebelling against her mother's control."

"Just like Sandy did with you."

Joanne laughed. "Soon as she started smelling herself, Sandy just knew she was grown."

When Quentin arrived at the house, Chuck escorted him to the library where Black was waiting. He wasted no time getting to the point of his visit. Black, as he always did, sat quietly and listened to what Quentin had to say, all the while wondering why he was telling him all this because absolutely none of it had anything to do with him nor The Family that he controlled. But he knew that Quentin would get around to the reason soon, at least he hoped he so.

"The reason I'm telling you all this is because yesterday, an FBI agent, Special Agent Connie Lewis, came to see me in my office."

Black held up his hand and frowned. "Just the words 'FBI' and 'special agent' make my stomach turn."

"It did more than just turn my stomach." He thought about Beason and his anger, but that could wait, at least until Beason got back from Zurich. "But I was thinking that if there's an investigation underway and they start following the money—"

"And they *always* do."

"Eventually, it's going to lead them to—"

"The fundraiser Beason held for Martin at the Rockville office," Black said.

"Right."

"How much money did he raise?" Black needed to know.

"He raised $35,000; twelve thousand of that was drawn on Rockville cashier's checks," Quentin said. "And whatever this mess is about, I know that Martin doesn't need Daniel's stink anywhere near him. Even if he returns the money, it'll still bc headline news."

"You're right," Black said. "Martin needs to get out in front of this before it becomes a story and return the money now."

"Won't that make Daniel look guilty of . . . of whatever this shit is when it comes out?"

"You think Martin will give a fuck?"

Quentin laughed. "No."

"I'll talk to Martin."

"Daniel said he'd be back today. I'm gonna find out what this was all about," Quentin promised.

Later that day, Chuck drove Black to meet Martin. He was doing a dedication at a women's center honoring Shirley Chisholm, the first African American woman elected to the United States Congress, the first African American, and the first woman to run for president of the United States. After his short speech, Martin's body man, Scotty, led him away from the press to a small room where Black was waiting.

"You know I hate it when you want to have these pop-up meetings," Martin said as he and Black shook hands. "It always means bad news on the horizon."

"I'm fine, Martin. How are you?"

Martin laughed. "I'm fine, but I guess that depends on why *you're* here."

"There's some type of investigation into Daniel Beason and his bank."

"Rockville something or other." Martin thought for a second. "He did a fundraiser for the campaign," he said, and Black was glad that he didn't have to remind Martin of the significance of it. "Scotty, see to it that we discreetly return that money to its donors."

"I'll take care of it."

"Anything else?"

"That's it. I knew that you'd want to get out in front of this before it became press-worthy," Black said and shook Martin's hand. Then he waited for him to leave before he and Chuck left the women's center and walked back to the Mercedes-Maybach.

"Where to, boss?" Chuck asked.

"Drop me off at Bobby's house, and then you can take the rest of the day off."

Chapter Twenty-five

The investigation into the death of Elias Colton had taken an unexpected turn that following morning when the fingerprint analysis came back from the lab. It had been established that the maid had cleaned the apartment on the morning of the murder. Therefore, all of the prints which were collected at the scene were fresh. Other than the deceased, there were three identifiable sets of prints.

One set was found in the bedroom as well as the bathroom. Those were believed to be the prints of Gayle Eager, who admitted being there that day. The other prints were found in the living room and the office. They were able to identify who one of the prints belonged to. Jack and Diane were confident that those were the prints of the killer. The fingerprints of their prime suspect, Albert Eager's prints, were in the system due to an arrest for DUI.

"We checked Eager's prints against the one we found at the crime scene," Detective Santiago reported.

"And?" Diane asked.

Santiago shook his head. "They weren't a match. But we *did* get a match."

"Were you waiting on a drumroll?" Jack asked.

"It's called a 'pause for dramatic effect.'"

"Forgive me," Jack said.

"The prints belonged to Daniel Beason." Santiago paused to enjoy the shocked looks on Jack and Diane's faces. "His prints were in the system because he was arrested five years ago and charged with assault."

Although she had no actual proof to speak of, Susan Beason had always believed that her husband, Daniel, had cheated on her with several women during their fifteen-year marriage, and that included prostitutes. The unanswered questions, the unexpected "business meetings," and the trips that she was never permitted to accompany her husband on all meant one thing to her—and she was right.

Daniel cheated on her, and she had accepted that long ago. Susan settled for the money and position that she'd always dreamed of. In those moments when she was honest with herself, she'd admit that was why she first became interested in a man on his third wife. Daniel Beason had money and position, and he wanted her, so she married him for his money and status. Although she had many moments of regret over her choice, Susan was living the life she wanted, albeit without sex, and she had learned to live without that.

But it was being left alone that Susan hated, and being lonely led to her beginning a friendship with a man named Amir Malachi, and it was just that . . . a friendship. And perhaps if the relationship had been left to its own devices and was allowed to develop to its logical conclusion, maybe Susan would have ended up in Amir's bed, but it never got that far.

One evening, Beason came home early from one of those "business trips" that he had taken with Alisha Grico, the assistant to somebody he was doing business with at the time, and found Susan in the bathtub talking to her would-be lover with the phone on speaker.

He stood listening to his wife talk of being tired of being left alone and wishing that her husband would pay more attention to her.

"I would never leave you alone the way he does. I'd be making love to you constantly," Amir said, and Beason covered his mouth to keep from laughing out loud.

But it was when he heard Susan say, "Maybe you should come get in this tub with me," that he rushed into the bathroom and knocked the phone out of her hand.

Beason jerked her out of the tub and slapped her repeatedly. She was able to get away from him when she ran, and he slipped on the water on the floor left from jerking Susan out of the bathtub. With Beason in pursuit, Susan ran out of the house naked to a neighbor's house, who took her in and called the police.

"He was arrested, but the wife wouldn't press charges," Santiago informed them.

"Guess that means we have a new prime suspect," Jack said and shook Santiago's hand. "Thanks for rushing this over."

"I didn't do it for you, Jack." He turned to Diane and took her hand in his. "Anytime *you* need something rushed over, Diane, you know I remain your loyal subject."

"Thank you, Diego," she said as Santiago kissed her hand.

"But you can call too, Jack," he said and walked off.

"So, let's go to see Mr. Beason and find out what he has to say," Diane said and left the precinct with Jack. However, when they arrived at the Beason home, Susan informed them that her husband was away on business in Switzerland.

Jack and Diane looked at each other.

"When do you expect him back, Mrs. Beason?" Diane asked.

"He should be back later this evening."

"Thank you, Mrs. Beason. We'll stop by later then," Jack said.

"Is there anything that I could help you with, Detective?" Susan asked, concerned.

"No, we just need to ask him a question," Jack replied and handed her a card. "Have Mr. Beason call us when he gets in this evening, please."

When Jack and Diane walked away from the house, both thought how convenient it was that he was out of the country.

"You think he'll call when he gets back?" Diane asked as they drove away from the house.

"No. I'm not even sure that he'll be back. But we'll be back anyway," Jack said, and they headed to the home of Elias Colton to talk to Cissy. The detectives intended to delicately confirm Gayle's story about Elias asking her for a divorce.

"Not that she'll tell us if he did," Diane said.

"She won't?"

"No."

"Why not? He's dead now. What difference does it make if it helps us catch her husband's killer?"

"Men." Diane shook her head. "Even if she knew about the affair . . . excuse me, *affairs,* and I think that she did, and even if it were true that he asked her for a divorce, what she has left is her pride, and she's not going to give that up."

However, in light of Albert and Gayle no longer being suspects, the more pressing issue that they wanted to talk to her about was Colton's relationship with Daniel Beason. But since it was on his mind, Jack asked Cissy anyway about their relationship, and as Diane told him to expect, Cissy said that she and Elias were doing fine.

"In fact," Cissy said and wiped away a tear, "we were planning our silver anniversary celebration."

"Once again," Diane said compassionately, "I am so sorry for your loss, Mrs. Colton. I can't imagine what you and the people closest to Mr. Colton must be feeling."

"Yes, it has been hard on everybody. I spoke with Quentin this morning. He's been very supportive throughout this ordeal."

"What about his other friends? How are they taking it?" Jack continued on the same line.

"I think we're all taking his loss badly. But Quentin and Danny, I think it's hitting them the hardest."

"Danny?" Diané questioned.

"Daniel Beason. As I told you, he and Elias have been friends for years."

"Have you heard from him?"

"I believe he's away on business. Zurich, I think that's where Susan said he was."

"Do you know if they were involved in some type of business together?"

"Elias and Danny were always into something, so I really couldn't say with any certainty what the two of them were involved in now. If it made money, those two were always all in."

"So, it wouldn't be unusual for Mr. Beason to have been in the apartment?"

"He was there all the time because they were close friends, and as I said, if it made money, Elias and Danny were all about that," Cissy reiterated.

"I think that we have all we need for now, Mrs. Colton," Diane said.

Jack and Diane stood up. "Thank you for your time, Mrs. Colton."

"Anything I can do to help, and it's Cissy, please." Cissy stood up. "But there is one more thing before you go."

"What's that?"

"Elias had a Surface Pro that's missing. That thing was like his right hand. He was *never* without it."

"Thank you, Mrs. Colton. If you can find the serial number for it, that would help us find it," Jack said, and the detectives left the house.

Now they had something else to ask Beason about. Since they had no confidence that he would call them when he got back—or *if* he were even coming back—Jack and Diane drove back to Beason's house and waited.

Just before nine that evening, Beason's Executive Flight Lines' flight from Paris touched down. Unfortunately, things didn't go the way he hoped and needed them to go in Zurich, and now he had the problems he'd hoped to avoid. He called for an

Uber, thinking that Colton's problems were now
his problems. Beason cursed Colton for his arro-
gance in believing that he could get the upper hand.
What was he going to do now? Beason had no idea,
but he knew that he was in deep shit.

It was just after ten when Beason arrived at his
house. Jack and Diane were waiting for him. They
watched as he went inside. First, the detectives
gave him ten minutes to kiss and tell lies to his
wife. Then once they thought he had enough time
for her to inform him about their earlier visit,
they got out of their car and rang the bell. Susan
answered the door and invited the detectives into
the living room where Beason was waiting, and
then she went upstairs and left them alone with
her husband. Diane immediately noticed the
troubled look on his face.

Because he's guilty was what that look told her.

"What can I do for you, Detectives?"

"Just a few questions to clarify some things,"
Jack said.

"Happy to help." Beason loosened his tie. "What
can I clear up for you?"

"When we first spoke, you said that the last time
you saw Mr. Colton before he was murdered was
earlier that day, correct?" Diane asked.

"That's right."

"Where was that, Mr. Beason?" Jack asked.

"At the apartment in the city."

"Where he was murdered?" Diane inquired.

"Was there a reason that you went to see him?" Jack asked.

"No reason in particular." He shrugged his shoulders and forced out a smile. "I was in the area, so I stopped by to see if he wanted to get a drink."

"What time was this?" Jack questioned.

"Oh, I'd say it was about five, five fifteen maybe."

"How long did you stay?" Jack asked.

"Not long. Elias said that he had an appointment coming, so we went down to the bar on the corner. We returned a little after six. I'm not sure of the time."

"What did you two talk about?" Jack inquired.

"The fundraiser for the organization."

"That would be the Association of Black Businesses?" Jack said.

"Right."

"Did you two ever do any business together?" Jack asked.

He chuckled nervously. "All the time."

"Anything going on now?" Jack pressed.

While her partner questioned Beason, Diane kept an eye on his facial expressions and body movements because they were telling her a different story than the one coming out of Beason's mouth.

"Nothing in particular at the moment."

"Okay." Diane paused and then took over the questioning. "You said that you went and had a drink with Colton sometime after five, and you were back sometime after six, but you can't tell me exactly what time, is that correct?"

"That's right."

"Can you tell me where you went after that?" Diane asked.

"After I left Elias, I returned to my office. I had a late meeting with Andrea Frazier, the COO at my company, and then I went home."

"What time did you get back to your office for this meeting with Ms. Booker?"

"It was a little after seven," Beason said. He had so many other things on his mind that it wasn't until that moment that he realized that the detectives were treating him like a suspect.

"And what time did the meeting with Ms. Booker wrap up?"

"I'm not exactly sure of the time, but it was sometime around nine thirty or nine forty-five, maybe."

"And what time did you get home?" Diane asked.

"It was sixteen minutes after ten."

"Exactly?"

"Yes, exactly."

"How can you be so sure of the time?"

"I noted the time when I turned off the alarm."

"And you have no knowledge of anyone that would want to kill Colton or why?" Diane pressed.

"No, Detective. I'm sorry, but I can't think of anybody that would want Elias dead. He was a good and decent man." Beason stood up. "Now, if you'll excuse me, it's late, and I've had a very long day. A long couple of days, in fact, and I'd like to get some rest and spend some time with my wife."

Jack and Diane stood up. "I completely understand. Sorry to have bothered you so late," Jack said and shook his hand.

"We'll be in touch soon, Mr. Beason," Diane said and turned to leave. *Because you did it,* she thought, and then she thought about what Black told her.

Albert and Gayle look good for it, but you think it's deeper than that. If you don't, you should.

Chapter Twenty-six

The following morning when Jack and Diane arrived at the precinct, they checked the recording from the building on the day of the murder before the malfunction. They saw Beason entering the building at five fifteen and leaving with Colton at five twenty-one, just as he said. Then Colton returned to the building alone at six ten.

"If he's walking in the building at six ten, I think it's safe to say that he was alive the last time Beason saw him," Diane said, and she and Jack began rethinking their theory of the crime.

"Where does that leave us?" Jack asked.

"Back to square one, I guess," Diane said and sank into her seat.

"Okay, let's take it from the top. What do we know for sure?"

"We know that Daniel Beason and Gayle Eager were both in the apartment at some point before the murder. Other than those two facts, all we have is speculation," Diane said. "Damn it, Jack, I just *knew* that it was Albert," she stated, and then she laughed.

"What?"

"Just something Mike Black said to me. It's been haunting me because I was so sure that Albert did it."

"What did he say?"

"He said, 'Albert and Gayle look good for it, but you think it's deeper than that. If you don't, you should.'"

Jack started laughing. "He said that?"

"Sure did."

"When were you gonna share *that* with me?"

"I didn't think I needed to. Albert and Gayle looked so good for it, and all the evidence was pointing their way."

"So let me get this straight. You go see a killer to ask his advice on killing, and he tells you that Albert and Gayle look good for it—"

"Which they did," Diane smiled.

"Then he says that you think it's deeper than that, which you didn't—"

"Nope." She shook her head. "I was stuck on my usual sex and money theory."

"And if you don't think it's deeper than that, or you're stuck on your usual sex and money theory, that you should. Am I getting this right, Diane?"

"Stupid of me, huh?"

"Yes, because, honestly," Jack began mimicking her voice, "and I mean you no disrespect, he knows more about murder than either of us, so you go to hear his insights. And then he gives you the very insight you seek—and you blow it off. Am I getting this right?"

"Yes, Jack. You're getting it right."

"Did you ask him *why* he thought it was deeper than that?"

"He said it was just a feeling," Diane answered, and Jack looked at his watch and stood up. "Where are you going?"

"Prestige Capital and Associates to ask Black what the feeling was based on."

Diane stood up. "I know I should have asked, but—"

"But you were stuck on your usual sex and money theory."

"And I'm usually right," she said. As they were about to leave, they received a report from the forensic accountant assigned to the case. The investigation revealed that according to Colton's financial records, there was business between Beason and Colton in the form of a significant investment in a company called the Rousseau Land Development that Beason didn't mention. And that, once again, changed everything for the detectives.

"Just because Beason left the building doesn't mean that he didn't come back," Diane said. "He could have just as easily come back when Jonathan was gone. Then he would have had plenty of time to have a drink, push Colton off the balcony, taken the tablet, came out with the rest of the crowd, and disappeared in the chaos."

"I like it. I say the first thing we do is verify his alibi. Talk to Susan and Andrea Frazier."

However, Jack and Diane weren't the only ones that wanted to see Andrea Frazier, and *he* had gotten to her first. When she got to the office later that morning, she was shocked to see Daniel Beason's car in the parking lot. *He never gets here this early,* Andrea thought and went into the building. Once inside, Andrea found Beason hard at work shredding documents.

Everything was coming apart at the time and closing in on him. Had he had any real sense, Beason would have gotten off his return flight when it touched down in Paris, liquidated as much of his assets as he could, and disappeared. But Beason always did think that he was smarter than everybody else, so he knew that he could fix it, make everything all right, and everyone could go back to business as usual. Then he came home . . . to find the police waiting for him. They all but accused him of murdering Elias Colton, and Beason thought he'd be walking out in handcuffs. But he would deal with that later. Right then, Connie Lewis was his most immediate problem, and that had to be dealt with first.

"I'd ask what you're doing, but I'm sure that I don't want to know," Andrea said, startling Beason when she walked up behind him.

"Andrea. Good. I'm glad you're here," Beason said as he put another stack of documents in the shredder.

"I'm not," she said and wished that she had stopped at The Muffin Man for coffee and a Banana Macadamia Muffin. If she had, maybe she wouldn't be standing there now about to—once again—become an accomplice to whatever Beason was shredding documents over.

"I need your help."

Before he left for Zurich, he had told her about what happened with Quentin and the investigation into the activities surrounding The Green Ridge Development Corporation. Once he mentioned Green Ridge, Andrea knew that this was about Rousseau Land Development's construction project that Beason was invested in and why he was shredding documents.

The thousand-acre property that Beason was developing was priced at about one point eight million dollars, which was more than Beason could afford to invest at the time. In addition, he could only borrow $60,000 from his savings and loan. Therefore, he used other methods to raise the additional funds. And *that* was where Andrea came in.

"What do you need me to do?" she asked and braced herself for the response.

"Talk to Donna. Make sure we're all on the same page with this. And be prepared to talk to Connie Lewis when she comes," Beason said and went back to shredding documents.

Andrea didn't say anything. She just nodded her acknowledgment and went to her office. She was glad that he didn't ask her to do anything else illegal, but what he told her was bad enough. She had just as much exposure on Rousseau, if not more. The thing to do now was to call Donna Smith, and they start protecting themselves. They were looking at bank fraud: a fine of up to a million dollars and possibly thirty years in prison. She watched from her window as Beason drove off before she picked up the phone to make her call to Donna Smith and told her what was going on.

Andrea had just gotten off the phone when her assistant informed her that the police were there to see her about the death of Elias Colton.

"Detectives," she said and came from behind her desk when they were shown in her office.

"Thank you for taking the time to see us," Jack said and shook her hand.

"I know that you have a lot to do, so I promise that we won't take up much of your time," Diane said, also shaking Andrea's hand.

"Please, have a seat. Can I get you anything?"

"No, thank you," Jack said as they sat down. "I only have one question. About your boss."

"What about Daniel?"

"On the night that Mr. Colton was murdered, Mr. Beason said that he had a late meeting with you. Could you tell me where that meeting took place, what time it began, and what time it ended?"

"Is Daniel a suspect?" Andrea wanted to know.

"We're just asking questions, Ms. Booker."

"Daniel got here a little after seven."

"And what time did the meeting end?"

"Let's see. I'm not sure what time we wrapped up, but I left here after ten that night, so it had to be sometime before that."

After thanking her for her time, Jack and Diane went to talk to his wife, Susan, and as expected, she also confirmed his story.

"But Susan seemed shaky to me. I think I'm gonna give her awhile to think about it, then double back and push her," Diane said as they drove away from the house.

"Sounds good."

"Without you, Jack."

"Oh. Okay. I'll get started on getting a subpoena for the security company for his home, his office, and the surrounding houses to verify what time he arrived. That sound good?"

"That sounds perfect," Diane said, and after dropping Jack off at the precinct, she doubled back on Susan Beason.

"Detective Mitchell?" Susan questioned, surprised to see her back and without her partner.

"Hello, Mrs. Beason. Do you mind if I come in?"

"Sure, why not?"

"Thank you," Diane said and went inside. Susan sat down in the living room and picked up a glass of wine.

"Can I get you one," she offered, holding up her glass.

"No, thank you. On duty."

"What can I do for you this time? You think I killed Elias?"

"No, Susan. Can I call you Susan?"

"You already did."

"No, Susan, I don't think you killed him."

"But you think Danny killed him."

Diane smiled her answer. "Funny thing is, I think that you think that Danny killed him too. Or you at least think that there's a possibility, don't you, Susan?"

She took a swallow. "What makes you think that?"

"You told us that he got home at sixteen minutes after ten, not a little after ten, not sometime around ten. You said that your husband got home at *exactly* sixteen minutes after ten, which is the exact time that Mr. Beason told you to say, isn't it, Susan?"

Susan said nothing.

"I saw the way that you looked at my partner when he asked you. The way that you looked away, then said it again, but with more confidence that time, like you needed him to know you were positive of the time."

Susan still said nothing.

"How many times has he asked you to lie for him?"

Susan remained silent.

"How many times has he lied to *you?*" Diane paused. "And he's lied to you so many times that you know a lie when you hear it."

Susan finished her wine and looked at Diane.

"So, you knew he was lying when he told you what time he got home."

"You're right. I do know when Danny's lying."

"But this lie isn't to cover up his being with some woman. This lie is for you to help him cover up a murder. That makes *you* an accessory to murder."

"I take Temazepam at night to help me get to sleep," Susan said without hesitation at the words "accessory to murder." All she heard Diane say was . . . "You're going to jail." "So I have no actual idea when Danny got home that night. The only thing that I can tell you for sure is that he was in bed when I woke up around four in the morning."

When Diane called Jack and told him what Susan had said, he agreed that they should go back to see Andrea Frazier and push her about the meeting and exactly what time Beason left her. However, when the detectives arrived at the offices of Rockville Guaranty Savings and Loan, they weren't the only ones who wanted to talk to Andrea Frazier.

"Detectives Harmon and Mitchell to see Andrea Frazier."

"Ms. Booker is in a meeting right now, but if you would have a seat, I will let her know you're here," the receptionist said, and the detectives sat down.

"Excuse me, Detectives. My name is Connie Lewis." She showed her badge. "I'm with the FBI, and as it happens, I'm here to see Ms. Booker too."

"Really?" Jack said, and Diane giggled.

"You tell us about yours, and we'll tell you about ours," Diane said.

"I'm here to speak with Ms. Booker because Mr. Daniel Beason and this fine institution are under investigation for bank fraud involving The Green Ridge Development Corporation and Rousseau Land Development, which somehow collapsed, despite earning over $2 million in commissions and fees. What about you?"

"We're investigating the murder of Elias Colton, and we're here to confirm Daniel Beason's alibi with Ms. Booker."

"Elias Colton . . . He was involved with Beason and Quentin Hunter in the Green Ridge fraud scheme," Connie said, and that began a discussion about what else their cases had in common. The vaunted words *interagency cooperation* were tossed around.

Connie stood up when Andrea Frazier's assistant came out and said that Ms. Booker was ready to see her. "You guys coming?" she asked.

And in the spirit of genuine interagency cooperation, Jack and Diane got up and accompanied her.

"You two again?" Andrea said.

"You just don't know how sorry we are that we have to keep coming back, Ms. Booker," Jack began. "But we just came from talking to Susan Beason, and I was wondering if there was anything about the statement you sat there earlier and gave me that you wanted to change?"

"Now, this is just me, Ms. Booker," Connie said. "But I would take advantage of the opportunity to amend your statement, if necessary. You know— since they just talked to the wife, and now they're back. If it were me, I'd be thinking about 'accessory after the fact.' But that's just me."

"Mr. Beason left my office at the time that I said, but I left the building alone almost thirty minutes later than that, and his car was gone."

Chapter Twenty-seven

It had been a couple of days, and there was still no sign of Rain's cousin, Sapphire. She had told Carter to handle it for her, but that was more to give him something to do other than hanging around her. Since he had gotten in the habit of just showing up unexpectedly at her house, Rain had moved to Wanda's safe house. Not only was her safe house better fortified and better stocked than Rain's, but also Carter had no idea where it was. She knew that at some point, they would have to have a conversation. After all, *you are pregnant with his baby,* but she wasn't feeling it.

Carter had put Geno and Chao on finding her, but they had come up empty so far. Rain had even enlisted Carla's help in the search, "Because if you can't find her, she ain't nowhere to be found," Rain confidently boasted.

However, she was disappointed when Carla said, "Sorry, Rain, but I guess she ain't nowhere to be found. But I'll stay on it," she promised.

"I know you will," Rain said and ended the call. She was just about to put down the phone when it rang. Thinking it was Carla calling back, she answered without looking at the display. "This Rain."

"Lorraine?" her aunt Priscilla questioned because she had heard the name before. She was the boss of Mike Black's criminal organization. *Everybody* heard of Rain Robinson.

"Yes, ma'am."

There was a brief silence. "You're *Rain* Robinson?" she asked gently because she had no idea.

"Yes, ma'am," Rain said softly, and there were a few more seconds of silence as Priscilla wondered why Millie never mentioned that Barbara's daughter was Rain Robinson.

"Have you found Sapphire yet?" she asked because that was what was important.

"No, ma'am. I'm sorry. I'm doing everything I can to find her, and I got my people out looking for her."

Priscilla took a deep breath and tried to put the best face on it. "She'll turn up. She always does. And she'll have some fantastic story about where she'd been and why she couldn't call," she said, but she was slowly losing hope.

"I hope so. But I'm gonna keep looking for her."

"Thank you, Lorraine." She paused. "The other reason that I called was to tell you that today is your cousin Judean's tenth birthday, and we're having a party for him at my house."

"Please wish him a happy birthday for me."

"I will, but I was hoping that you might want to come and that you would bring Lakeda and her children with you."

"I don't know," Rain hesitated, "Aunt Priscilla." She felt a little uncomfortable saying it.

"I understand your reluctance, but I think they should know their family, Lorraine, and you should too."

"I can't make any promises for Lakeda and the kids."

"I understand that too. But I just want you to think about coming."

"Yes, ma'am," Rain said respectfully. "I will think about it."

"Thank you. Hopefully, I'll see you tonight," Aunt Priscilla said, and she hung up the phone thinking about all the things she'd heard about her niece, Rain Robinson.

The second that Rain hung up the phone, she knew that she wasn't going, but the seed had been planted. *They should know their family, Lorraine, and you should too*. Therefore, later that night, Rain was sitting in the living room at Millie's house telling Lakeda, Miles Junior, and Rasheeda about their family.

"Honestly, Aunt Rain, I didn't think you had a mother," Miles Junior said.

"What you think? I was created in a lab somewhere?"

"No," Rasheeda said. "It's just that you never talk about her, just Grandaddy."

"I know. That's because I never really knew my mother. She died when I was young," Rain said and told them the story.

"You think Mr. Jasper killed them?" Lakeda asked, and Rain stared at her without speaking because, to her thinking, Lakeda knew *precisely* what her father-in-law was capable of doing.

"You knew him. What *you* think?"

Lakeda thought about it. When she found out that her husband, Miles, was having an affair with Tatiana Phillips, she told Jasper about the matter, and he sent men to kill her. It was the reason that Miles was in jail. "Yeah, he killed them."

"Damn," Miles Junior said. "Grand Pops was a treacherous nigga."

"I think we should go," Rasheeda said because she, more than her brother, had always felt like they were alone in the world. "They're our family, and we should get to know them."

"I don't. Grand Pops killed their sister. We ain't gonna be welcome there," Miles Junior said.

"They *did* invite us," Lakeda said because she wanted to go too.

She never knew her family. Lakeda had grown up in the system, bouncing from group home to group home. So the only family that she'd ever known was sitting in that room.

"*One* person invited us. Maybe *she* wants us there, but what about the rest of them?" Miles Junior asked.

"What do you think we should do, Millie?" Lakeda questioned. As she had been to Rain, Millie had become like a mother to her too.

"I think y'all should have an opportunity to get to know your family. Whether they accept you is up to them. But you will always be able to say that you tried."

"So, we're going, right?" Rasheeda asked, looking at her brother, and he nodded.

"Good. Y'all have a good time," Millie said. "But I'm not going."

"Why not?" Rasheeda asked.

"They know Blue was the one who told Jasper about them the night she got killed. Those people hate me too."

"Oh yes, the fuck you *are* going. Only reason I took my black ass over there in the first place was that you told me to. So, yeah, Millie, your black ass *is* going," Rain said and stood up. "We all are. Get dressed," she said, walking out of the room.

"I guess she settled that," Miles Junior stated.

"Doesn't she always," Rasheeda said, and they all got up to get ready to go to the Langston family home to celebrate the tenth birthday of Judean, the fourth son of Brayden Langston, the oldest of the Langston clan. He hated Jasper the most for murdering his baby sister.

Priscilla was happy to get Rain's call that she would come and that Lakeda, Miles Junior, Rasheeda, and Millie were coming with her. *That was the easy part,* she thought, then dialed Brayden's number. It was his son's party, so he had a right to know who she had invited.

"Why the fuck would you do that?" he shouted.

"Because she is our niece, and they are our family. None of them had *anything* to do with what Jasper did!" Priscilla shouted back, so it was shaping up to be an interesting evening at the Langston family home.

On the way to Aunt Priscilla's house, a discussion of Rain's security came up. She decided that she wouldn't wear her vest, but the question was, what to do with her guns?

"What you want us to do?" Ricky asked as he drove.

"Y'all wait outside," Rain said.

Alwan shook his head. "No."

"Fuck you mean no?"

"I mean no. Carter said that I shouldn't let you outta my sight," Alwan insisted.

"If he was so concerned about Rain, he wouldn't have fucked Fantasy," Ricky said softly.

"Shut up," Alwan said quickly.

"Wait, what?"

"Nothing," Ricky said. "I didn't say—"

"Shut up, Ricky. Alwan, what's he talking about?"

He looked at Ricky. "Asshole." Alwan looked back at Rain. "Carter left the after-fight party with Fantasy."

Rain didn't say anything for the rest of the trip to Aunt Priscilla's house. But what she had just heard stayed on her mind. *If he was so concerned about Rain, he wouldn't have fucked Fantasy.* Although it hurt Rain to hear it, hearing it forced her to think about things she already knew but had chosen to overlook because she was fucking him. There were things that she had decided not to think about because she was pregnant with his baby.

Carter Garrison was *not* the man for her. He was suitable for the purpose he served, but he could never be her man. For one, she didn't love him. Rain loved the way that he fucked her. And then there was the fact that Carter was still and always would be in love with Mileena.

When Ricky parked the car, Alwan got out to open Rain's door. She climbed out and waited until Lakeda, Miles Junior, Rasheeda, and Millie got out of their car.

"Ricky, you wait out here. Alwan, you're with me," she said, and they walked toward the house.

Alwan pointed in Ricky's face. "Me and you gonna talk about how you fucked up today," he said and rushed to catch up with Rain.

"Y'all ready?" Rain asked and turned to Alwan. She took a deep breath and hoped she was making the smart move when she handed him her guns.

"You gonna be all right, Aunt Rain?" Rasheeda asked because she had just witnessed something that she'd never seen before.

"Alwan is here with me." She looked at him, and he nodded. "I'll be fine," Rain said and rang the doorbell as the tension began to build. As she waited, Rain wondered if the tension was because she would meet her family or because she had just given up her guns.

When Priscilla opened the door, she was thrilled to see Rain, Lakeda, Miles Junior, and Rasheeda, and Priscilla was surprised when Millie walked in behind them. Rain introduced her to everybody. She was happy to see Millie again after all those years. Excited, Priscilla invited them into her home and into the room where Judean's birthday party was going on.

"Hey, everybody," Priscilla said loud enough to get their attention. "There're some people that I want you all to meet." She put her arm around Rain. "This is Barbara's daughter, Lorraine, and this is her son, Miles's wife, Lakeda, and her children, Miles Junior and Rasheeda."

The reaction in the room was mixed.

Some people were glad to meet their long lost family, and they welcomed their new family members with open arms. Others, not so much.

"Glad to finally meet you."

"Welcome to the family."

Those other family members, Brayden, Vincent, and Evangelia, in particular, believed that Jasper had killed their sister, and they were disgusted that these people had the nerve to be there and were mad at Priscilla for bringing them there.

"I don't know why you thought this was cool," Vincent said to his sister.

"Don't be like that, Vincent," Charlene pleaded. She and Elliot had always been more understanding about the situation than their siblings. But Vincent wasn't hearing it.

He gathered up his wife and children and left.

"I'm sorry, Priscilla. I know you meant well, but it's how some of us feel," Evangelia said. "I'm staying, but only because it's Judean's birthday."

However, others at the party knew *exactly* who Barbara Robinson's daughter was, and they were scared because the name "Rain Robinson" carried weight in the streets.

"Fuck that Lorraine shit. That's Rain Robinson," one young man said after being introduced.

But for the most part, everybody was polite and well behaved, and everybody, including Rain, was having a good time. She and Rasheeda enjoyed listening to Uncle Elliot, her aunts Priscilla, Charlene, and even Evangelia tell old stories and share happy memories of their sister. It was good to hear someone say nice things about the mother she never got the chance to know . . . The kind of person she was, what she liked and loved, and how she had touched each of their lives in a special way. It took Rain's mind off the words, *if he was so concerned about Rain, he wouldn't have fucked Fantasy* . . . at least for a little while.

Meanwhile, outside the house, Ricky had noticed a car parked down the street, and the people inside hadn't gotten out. So he took out his phone and made a call.

Alwan was trying to give Rain space and protect her at the same time, so he had gotten into a conversation with Rain's uncle Elliot's daughter, Anissa, and they were standing where he could see and get to Rain with her guns quickly. "Would you excuse me?" he asked, stepped away, and swiped talk.

"What's up?" he answered.

"Come outside."

"I'm on my way," he said and went to talk to Rain.

Once he had told her where he was going, Alwan went outside to see what Ricky wanted. "What's up, asshole?"

"Why I gotta be an asshole?"

"Telling her that shit about Carter wasn't cool. That's why you're an asshole, asshole. Now, what's up?"

"You see that silver Malibu parked five cars down on the right?" Ricky pointed.

"I see it. What about it?"

"Whoever it is in that car hasn't got out."

"How long they been sitting there?"

"I didn't see when they parked, so I can't say for sure, but they been there awhile."

"Okay. You keep your eyes on them. I'll let Rain know what's up," he said and went back into the house to find her.

Once Alwan had alerted Rain to the presence of men outside the house, she went to find Lakeda and Millie. After telling them what was up, she told them to stay and have a good time and was about to leave the party when Priscilla caught her at the door.

"You're not leaving already, are you, Lorraine?"

"Yes, Aunt Priscilla, I have to go," she said. Knowing that the men outside had bad intentions, she couldn't allow that to touch her family. "Lakeda, Millie, and the kids are gonna stay, but there's something that I need to take care of."

"I understand." She hugged Rain. "I hope this isn't gonna be the last time I see you, Lorraine."

"No, ma'am. I'll see you soon," Rain hugged her back, "when I find Sapphire and bring her home."

Priscilla smiled. "You be safe out there in them streets." She paused and shook her head. "Rain Robinson, my niece."

"Shhh." Rain put her finger over her lips and opened the door. Alwan was standing there waiting.

"Where are they?" she asked as Alwan handed her guns to her, and they walked back to the car.

"Silver Malibu, five cars down on the right," Ricky said and led the way to the car. Alwan opened the back door for Rain, and once he got in, Ricky drove off.

Rain looked back. "Here they come."

"Where you want to go?" Alwan asked.

"Just drive."

"You want me to lose them?" Ricky asked.

"No, just drive."

"Who you think they are?" Alwan asked.

"I think it's somebody looking for Fire," Ricky said.

"I'll try to remember to ask who they are before we kill them," Rain stated and began thinking about how she would ambush her pursuers. "Go to the new spot."

"What new spot?" Ricky asked, and Alwan told him how to get there.

With the success of Purple, the restaurant and lounge that Rain was partners with, along with Mileena and Yarrisa, they had talked about opening a second location and calling it Deep Purple. While she and Alwan were out one day, Rain had found a restaurant that had recently closed. She arranged to look at it the next day. Once Rain saw it, she thought it would be perfect for the new spot, so she bought it. With all that had been going on, especially with her fucking Carter and now being pregnant with his baby, Rain hadn't gotten around to telling her partners yet.

When they arrived at the spot, Rain and her men stood outside and waited to give their pursuers a chance to catch up. The minute she saw them turn the corner, she said, "There they are." They went inside and set up the ambush. Once inside, the silver Malibu parked, and four white men got out. Once they had checked their weapons, they entered the building to find Rain standing in the middle of the room.

"Who the fuck are you muthafuckas?" she asked, raised both of her weapons, and opened fire.

Rain made her way toward the bar for cover, firing shots along the way. As she ran, Alwan came up firing from behind the bar. Ricky was behind some tables on the other side of the lounge. When the pursuers turned to return Alwan's fire, Ricky stood up and began firing his Sig MPX 9 mm.

As they continued firing at Rain, she flipped over a table for cover and fired back, hitting one of the gunmen with three shots. Alwan and Ricky kept firing, and their engagement forced the other three gunmen to seek better cover. Once they were set, the three men blanketed the club with bullets. When one of the gunmen stood up, Alwan fired twice, hitting him with one to the chest and one to the head. Another fired and hit Ricky with two shots, but he kept firing at the gunman, hitting him with several shots until he went down.

Rain watched as the gun slipped from Ricky's hand, and he fell to the floor.

When the last gunman came out from cover and tried to run, he fired at Rain, but he missed her. She raised her weapons, fired, and hit him with several shots to the chest. He immediately fell over a table. Rain rushed to Ricky.

"Call Tammy and Rico!" she shouted.

"I'm already on it," Alwan yelled with the phone in his hand as he came from behind the bar and rushed to Rain and Ricky.

"You all right?" she asked Ricky, and then she looked at his wounds. He had taken one to the stomach and one to the chest. Both wounds were bleeding badly.

"I'll be all right, Rain," he said and tried to move.

"Don't move." Rain held him tighter. "Tammy and Rico are on their way."

"Did we get them?"

"Yeah, we got them," Alwan said.

"Hold on, Ricky." His body shook. "It's gonna be all right," she said, but Rain knew that all she could do was hold her loyal soldier until he had taken his last breath.

Chapter Twenty-eight

Joslin's breasts seemed to glisten, and her nipples grew harder as Marvin ran his tongue across them. He kissed her lips and kissed his way down her body, lingering at the nipples. He continued working his way south, crawled between her legs, spread her lips, and then slid his tongue inside her. He tongued her clit, and she grabbed his head to hold it in place while she screamed.

Suddenly, Joslin got up on her knees and started kissing his chest, his stomach, and finally, his dick. She stroked it, kissed it, ran her tongue along the length of it before taking it into her mouth, and began to suck. She glanced up at him as she opened her mouth and took him whole. Joslin's lips and tongue were soft and wet, and she could feel him begin to swell and his body quiver.

"Oh yeah, suck that dick just like that," he said softly and shoved himself deeper into her mouth.

Joslin stopped. "Shhh."

"Sorry."

She teased his head with her tongue and then slowly worked her way down. Joslin relaxed the muscles in her throat so she could take more of him into her mouth. She stroked and sucked furiously, and she felt him expanding in her mouth.

She took his head back in her mouth and continued to stroke him with both hands. Then Joslin began to fondle his balls with one hand and stroked him with the other, squeezing his balls lightly. After that, she let go and took him deep into her mouth and sucked it until he came.

Joslin smiled at the job she had done before they both passed out for a while, but she woke up shortly after that, got out of bed, and went into the bathroom. Marvin woke up when he heard the shower come on. He sat up in bed, and for a brief second or two, he considered getting out of bed and joining her, bending her sexy ass over and going up in her again. But the decision was made for him when he heard the water shut off.

Suddenly, the bathroom door swung open, and Joslin came rushing out naked and wet. She grabbed the bag she'd brought along with her and tossed it on the bed. Once she had pulled out the red, square neck, cutout back minidress, she picked up her purse and rushed back into the bathroom.

"So much for that idea," Marvin said and lay back down.

"Did you say something?" Joslin shouted from the bathroom.

"No," he shouted back.

Five minutes later, Joslin came out of the bathroom, dressed, hair and makeup done.

"I'm meeting Terri and Cha'relle at Club Constellation, and I'm late," she said, stepping into a pair of red Balenciaga patent leather, point-toe pumps. She reached in her bag and pulled out a red clutch. "You mind if I leave that bag here?"

"No."

"Can I come back after I leave the club?"

"If I'm here."

"I'll call first," Joslin said, leaning in to kiss him on the cheek before heading for the door.

When the door closed, Marvin was alone.

He turned on the television and flipped channels for a while, but nothing caught his attention. Therefore, it didn't take very long before his idle mind eased into thoughts of Sataria and the video she'd sent him. Earlier that day, Marvin received a text message from her that contained a link. He started to delete the message right away, but that was when Savannah Russell came into Healthy Lifestyle, the fitness center that he owned, and Marvin put the phone away.

When he tapped the link, more out of curiosity than anything else, Sataria's beautiful face appeared on his screen.

"Hello, Marvin. Since you won't talk to me, this is the only way I can say what I need to say. I love you, and I need to explain what actually happened, but I don't even know if you'll listen to this or delete it or just ignore it like you're ignoring me."

Marvin watched a single tear roll down her cheek, and it was as if he could feel the pain she was feeling, and maybe he could. Before all this happened, he was in love with her, and he felt closer to her than any woman before her.

Sataria quickly wiped the tear away. "I understand why you don't want to talk to me. You're hurt . . . I hurt you . . . So I understand why you won't talk to me and don't want to see me. But that's why we need to talk because I'm hurting too, and I know it's my fault. I did this to us. And that's why I need to explain to you what really happened. So I hope that you hear me out, and after you hear what happened, maybe you'll be able to forgive me."

Sataria repositioned herself in the chair and took a deep breath before she said, "I love you. I mean that. That is the one thing that I never lied about is that I love you so much. But I did lie to you . . . I kept things from you . . . things that I should have been honest with you about. Yes, I was married to George Andrews before I was married to Serek, and he cheated on me. I found out about the affair when the woman came to our apartment and said she was my husband's 'other woman.' When I told my cousin, Anita, about it, Cleavon and Zo did what they said they did, but I didn't tell them to do it. They went looking for him and got into a fight at the pool. And it just happened, but it wasn't because I told them to kil—to do that to him. Then when I got the insurance money, Cleavon started blackmailing me. He said that he would go to the police and tell them that I paid them to do that to George, so I paid him what he wanted, and I left Jacksonville and tried to put it all behind me."

"That doesn't explain you getting me to kill Serek," Marvin said to the screen as if she could hear him.

"I know that doesn't have anything to do with you. You want to know about Serek."

"Damn right I do."

"Okay, okay," she repeated and once again adjusted her position in the chair. "I fell in love with you the day I met you. You remember how sad and unhappy I was being with him. He ignored me, cheated on me just like George did, disrespected me for years, and then he started beating me. You know all that. And then I met you, and you made me so happy. I fell in love with you. You were so nice to me, and you treated me with so much respect, like I was your precious jewel. And I love

you so much, and all I want to do is be with you,"
Sataria said, and now her tears flowed.

"I never meant for what happened to happen,"
she said, wiping away her tears. "I didn't plan it.
I know how that tape made it sound, but I didn't
plan it. Anita recorded that because, at the
time, she had a restraining order against Cleavon,
and she was recording him threatening her. You
have to believe me, baby. She recorded that long
before . . . what happened, happened. Anita was
talking about Cleavon and how he was harass-
ing her at her job and coming to the house at all
hours of the night. And I was bragging, talking
shit about the amazing man that just walked into
my life, and I fell in love with him. That's the truth,
Marvin. I hope you believe me. Believe that I love
you, and I'm sorry that I did this to us. I should
have told you about Cleavon the second he walked
into Pesce and threatened me, but I was scared. I
was scared of what you think of me." Sataria began
to cry again. "I can't even imagine what you must
think of me now . . . I'm sorry . . . I can't do this—"

The video ended abruptly.

Marvin sat there for a few seconds before he let
it drop out of his hand. He did love Sataria, so it
hurt him to see her cry. *It's your weakness. You
never could stand to see her cry.* Her tears were
what set him off to kill Serek. He sat there looking

at the phone on the bed and thinking about what she said. The more he thought about it, the more he believed it. At least the backstory was true.

Marvin picked up the phone and was about to call her, but then he thought if the backstory were true, and if her words, *I can get that man to do anything I want him to do for me,* were true, did he want to continue the relationship?

Marvin put down the phone. He could almost hear her words, and it made him mad.

"Would you kill him? Not wait until he tries to kill me again. Would you kill him before he kills me and not after I'm dead?"

Just then, someone knocked at the door. That snapped Marvin out of his thoughts. "Who is it?"

"It's BC," Baby Chris shouted, and Marvin got out of bed, put on some pants, and went to open the door.

"What's up?"

"We got work to do. Jackie's downstairs."

"What's up with that?"

"I don't know. Jackie ain't in the best mood tonight, so I didn't ask. All she said to me was 'Come on,' and 'Where's Marvin?'"

"Fiona or Travis?" Marvin asked as he got dressed.

"I'm thinking it's Travis since Fiona was at the club with her."

"You're right. When they go at it, Fiona doesn't come to the club."

"And she was there." Baby Chris paused and shook his head. "The shit she had on tonight . . ."

"What's she wearing?"

That night, Fiona came to Conversations wearing a black satin Alexandre Vauthier deep V-neck ruffled minidress.

"But it ain't what she's wearing. It's how she looks in it. Shit, nigga, Fiona could wear a fuckin' Hefty garbage bag, and she'd look hot."

"I know *that's* right," Marvin said once he was ready.

"Look, Money . . . I just want to say that . . . you know . . . I know shit got you fucked up right now and shit," Baby Chris paused. "Damn, this shit is hard. But . . . What I'm trying to say is that I'm here for you, man. Whatever you need, you know," Baby Chris tapped his chest. "I got you."

"Yeah, that was hard, hard to listen to," he chuckled. "But thanks, brother. I appreciate it. I'll be all right," Marvin said, and they left the room.

"I know you will. I see you're already on the road to recovery."

Marvin pressed the button for the elevator. "How's that?"

"The only way to get over your woman is to replace her with three or four new ones," Baby Chris said as the elevator came and they got on.

"And?" Marvin asked, but that was his plan, and he would start with Savannah Russell and hoped to include LaSean Douglas in that mix.

"And I passed little sexy in the hot red dress on my way in. She said she put it on for you, so I should hurry before you pass out and don't hear the door," Baby Chris said as they walked through the lobby and left the hotel.

"Her sexy ass got some skills, but you see, I'm still standing, ready to put in work for my captain," Marvin said, and they got into the car with Jackie.

Chapter Twenty-nine

"What's up, boss?" Marvin said.

"Drive, and I'll tell you on the way," Jackie replied. Baby Chris started the car. "We're going to talk with some niggas that don't know how to listen."

"Who we talking about?" Baby Chris asked, if for no other reason than Jackie hadn't told him where to go.

"I'm tired of niggas thinking what I say is optional."

"Who?"

"Archie Smith and James Oliver."

"What they do?" Baby Chris asked.

"Does it matter?" Marvin said.

When Honey came to Conversations the night that Rain was there, it wasn't her first time coming there to complain about Archie Smith and James Oliver. After her first visit, Jackie sent Marvin and Baby Chris to talk with them. Baby Chris went to see Archie Smith and told him to back off Honey. Smith told Baby Chris that it must be some kind of misunderstanding between him and Honey because he wasn't trying to push her out.

"Good. Then we never have to have this conversation again, right?"

"No, BC, it's all good. Me and Honey ain't got no problem that we can't work out," Smith assured him. And Marvin had a similar talk with James Oliver. He too swore to Marvin that he and Honey were cool.

"You know me better than that, Money. I ain't that kind of muthafucka." He chuckled. "That's her spot now. I got mine."

Marvin pointed in his face. "Make sure." So the fact that they were going to talk to him *again* only proved to piss off Marvin. *Muthafucka,* he said to himself.

But their harassment of Honey continued, and that brought about her second visit. That was the night Rain was there, and Honey regretted not telling her what was going on even after Rain told her to let her know. On the way back to her spot, Honey imagined Rain showing up at Glover's with both of her guns drawn and walking up to Archie Smith and shooting him in the eye. And when James Oliver tried to run, *like the fuckin' coward he is,* Rain would shoot him in the back, walk up to him, and put two more in him. *That's* what she wanted to see, but there was a thing called chain of command, and Jackie was her captain.

After that visit, Jackie called each one to Conversations, and each assured their captain that they would stay out of Glover's and leave Honey to run her business.

"But the muthafuckas stood there and lied to my face," Jackie said angrily because earlier that evening, she got a call from Honey. She had just gotten off the phone with Travis. He was still in Juba, the capital of South Sudan, where he was overseeing a security contract for Nick's company. She asked him when he was coming home. He asked her to move to Juba, and their usual argument began. Therefore, when she got the call from Honey about Oliver and Smith back at her spot fuckin' with her when they swore to Jackie that they'd stay out of there, Jackie saw blood.

"So where we going?" Baby Chris asked.

"Where the nigga shouldn't be," Jackie said, and Baby Chris drove to Glover's.

When they arrived there, Marvin got out and opened Jackie's door. She got out, looked up at the sign flashing *Glover's*, and told Marvin to see that the sign was replaced with one that said *Honey's*. "And I want it up by tomorrow," Jackie said as Baby Chris held the door open for her, and she walked in what would soon be called Honey's.

The first person that Jackie saw when she came in was Archie Smith. He was standing at the bar having a drink with a rather attractive young lady.

Jackie started for him, taking out one of her guns as she walked. However, Baby Chris got a little ahead of her and reached Smith first. He tapped Smith on the shoulder.

"Your captain wants to see you."

When Smith turned around, Jackie shot him in the forehead.

She looked around the club. All eyes were glued on her.

"That's what happens to muthafuckas who can't follow orders," she said as Honey came rushing out of the back. Once she pushed her way through the crowd, she saw Smith's body on the floor with a bullet in his brain. She paused to savor the moment before she told two of her men to dispose of the body.

"The name of this place is Honey's," Marvin said as Jackie holstered her gun and walked toward the door. "You see what happens to dumb muthafuckas that think different."

Their next stop was the home of James Oliver. When they got there, Oliver had company over, and things were just starting to get heavy. That evening, he and Earvin Coolidge, who everyone called Cool, an up-and-coming member of Jackie's crew, were entertaining Shaleigh Howard and Brayonna Allen when Marvin banged on the door.

"Whoever it is needs to get the fuck outta here before they get shot up in this bitch!" Oliver shouted and kissed Brayonna.

Marvin banged on the door again. "It's your captain!" he shouted. "Now open the fuckin' door."

Oliver quickly pushed Brayonna off his lap and ran to the door to let them into the apartment. Jackie walked in first, followed by Marvin and Baby Chris. Jackie looked around at the ladies, and then she glanced at Baby Chris.

"Okay, ladies, the party is over," he said. "Get your shit and get out."

By that time, Marvin was standing in front of Oliver, who was trying to avoid eye contact.

"What's wrong?" Cool asked, putting on his shirt.

"This ain't got shit to do with you, Cool, so you need to go too," Baby Chris said.

"No," Jackie said quickly. "He stays," she said, thinking that there was a lesson about to be taught, and he needed to learn it too. Just not the way that Oliver was about to experience it.

He sat down. Silence filled the room as the ladies put on their clothes. As soon as they were dressed, Baby Chris escorted them to the door. The second he closed it, Marvin punched Oliver repeatedly in the face.

"I told you," Marvin hit him again, "then Jackie told you . . ." Marvin reached back and punched him again. This time, Oliver went down from the force of the blow. Marvin stood over him, kicked him in the face, and then repeatedly stomped Oliver about his head, shoulders, and back. "But dumb-ass niggas like you don't listen."

He grabbed Oliver, pulled him to his feet, reached back, and hit him again. Then Marvin picked up Oliver and threw him to the floor. When he got to his feet, Marvin hit Oliver with blow after blow until Oliver crumbled again. Finally, Marvin stood over him and kicked him a few more times as Cool eased over to Baby Chris.

"What's this about?" he asked softly so that Jackie wouldn't hear him.

"You heard the man. This is what happens when dumb-ass niggas don't listen to what their captain says."

Cool nodded and glanced over at Jackie. She had taken a seat and was watching her soldier put in work for her. Marvin pulled Oliver up from the floor and rammed him face-first into the wall. After that, he slammed Oliver's body into that same wall over and over again until Oliver went down. After that, Marvin stood over him and began to stomp Oliver once more.

Then Marvin got on top of him and hit Oliver several times in the face. He grabbed both sides of Oliver's head and began pounding it into the floor. Slowly, Marvin got to his feet and kicked Oliver in the face again before he pulled him up and slammed him into a wall. Oliver's face was a bloody mess as Marvin continued to ram his face into the wall, and when he let him go, he slumped to the floor. Oliver was dazed, but Marvin wasn't finished with him. He pulled him to his feet, hit him with lefts and rights to his face, and then threw a punch to the stomach that took all the wind out of Oliver. He totally collapsed. The beating was brutal—so brutal that Baby Chris was about to stop him, but Jackie grabbed his arm.

"Let him go. He needs this," she said, and she and Baby Chris watched as Marvin looked around for something else to beat Oliver with. Then he picked up a metal barstool and stood over Oliver, who tried to cover his head as Marvin hit him over and over again until he finally stopped moving. Marvin was covered in blood as he dropped the chair and stood over the helpless man.

Baby Chris checked for a pulse. "He's dead, Money."

Chapter Thirty

"I gotta feel this dick," Diane said softly and sighed as she eased herself down on it. She rode him slowly while he continued to feast on her nipples. Jack began to feel her legs trembling on his thighs, and he pushed harder. Finally, she bore down on him and increased her pace. She started pounding her hips furiously onto him until she reached a very loud and violent climax.

"Sorry, but I had to feel that dick in me," she said as she collapsed on his chest.

"Don't be," he managed. "And as soon as my heart stops pounding, I'll go make you pancakes."

"With eggs and bacon," Diane breathed out, but shortly after she said it, his hands were all over her body. They went from her breasts to her hips, her ass, and back up to her breasts again, and they went at it once more. Jack kissed her, nibbled her chin, sucked her neck, rolled her on her back, and then pushed her legs open. He dove into that wet pussy as if it were the greatest thing that he had ever experienced, and that was because it was. Diane started rocking her hips into him.

"Come hard for me," she demanded. "I want to feel you explode inside me."

Jack held her tighter and matched her stroke for stroke until he felt himself begin to expand inside her. Diane bit her bottom lip to keep herself from screaming. He fucked her, moving in and out of her faster and harder. Finally, Diane came, and they collapsed in each other's arms once again.

It was after ten when the detectives got to the precinct and were immediately presented with the security footage they had requested. They needed to track what time Daniel Beason left his office on the night of the murder and when he arrived home.

"Okay," Diane said as she cued up the footage from his office to the date and time. "There's Andrea Frazier."

"Exactly when she said. Do you see Beason's car anywhere?"

Diane paused the recording so they could take their time scanning the parking lot. "No, I don't see his car."

"I don't either."

"So let's back it up thirty minutes to the time Booker said that he left her office," Diane suggested, and she rewound the footage.

"Got him," Jack said excitedly when he saw Beason come out of the building and walk quickly to his car. "Note the time," he said when Beason got in and pulled off.

"Nine twenty-three," Diane said. "That gives him plenty of time to get from there to Colton's apartment to kill him."

"We need to get the footage from his house to know what time he arrived home."

"He filed an injunction to keep his monitoring service from releasing it."

"That's screams 'I'm guilty.'"

"Don't it," Diane said. "I can call Judge Peterson to expedite a warrant."

"But we are still going to need to place him at the scene at the time of the murder, or Judge Peterson will think we're just fishing," Jack said, But despite that, he felt like they were a step closer to closing their case. "We also need to establish a motive."

"Which brings us back to the missing tablet Cissy told us about."

"Any luck on pawnshops?"

Diane laughed. "No, and I wasn't expecting any. Whoever stole it, stole it for the information that was on it, not to pawn it for a couple of bucks."

"What do you think is on it?"

"My guess at this point, and the way this has been going for us, so it's just a guess, but based on what Special Agent Lewis told us, it's about this Rousseau land deal that he and Beason were involved in."

"So, what do we do now?" Jack asked, and Diane leaned forward.

"We could go to my place, you know, because it's closer, and we could pick up where we left off this morning. What do you think?"

"It will help clear our heads."

"Yes," Diane stood up. "Right." She pointed at Jack. "Clearer heads solve crimes," she said, and the detectives left the precinct in a hurry.

Like Jack and Diane, Quentin had love on his mind that morning. He had been sitting at his desk and not getting a damn thing done. But he didn't seem to care. Quentin had spent another amazing night making love to her, and it was wonderfully slow and passionate lovemaking. But it was the love they shared that morning that stayed on his mind.

"Good morning, beautiful," Quentin said as he entered her slowly and gently.

"Good morning," Ebony said, receiving his length and wrapping her arms and legs around him.

His pace was slow and constant as he slid in and out of her, wanting to feel every sensation her warmth had to offer. She kissed his neck and chest, loving the way he felt inside her. Then his movements accelerated, and she began rocking her hips into his. Ebony was amazing.

She was so wet for him that it made Quentin plunge deep inside her. It felt so good to him that he wanted to make it last. Her mouth and eyes opened wide, and she grabbed his face and kissed him passionately.

"Excuse me, Quentin."

"Yes, Samantha?" he said to his personal assistant to snap him out of his Ebony-induced fantasy.

"I have Special Agent Lewis here to see you."

"Really? She's the last person I wanted to see this morning," he said for more reasons than her interruption of his Ebony Fantasy.

He had hoped to hear from Beason before he talked to her again, but he hadn't. However, he had spoken to Susan, so he knew that Beason had gotten back from Switzerland the day before. So, after leaving messages on his cell and office phones, Quentin called and left messages with a few of Beason's lady friends, including Abony Shamone, a dominatrix that Beason spent time with. *If that's what you want to call it.* "Give me five minutes, then bring her in."

Before Samantha escorted Lewis into the office, Quentin tried calling Beason again on his cell and the direct line in his office and still got no answer. So then he called the house and spoke to Susan once again. Instead of telling Quentin that the police thought Beason killed Colton and she felt that he had probably left the country by then, she told him that she didn't know where he was or what was going on with him. Ever since she heard Diane say "accessory to murder," Susan had been trying to put some distance between them. She really didn't know what was going on, and she wasn't willing to go to jail for something she knew nothing about.

There was a light knock on the door. "I have Special Agent Lewis to see you, Mr. Hunter," Samantha said and escorted her in.

Quentin stood up and buttoned his jacket. "Thank you, Samantha. Please, have a seat, Ms. Lewis."

"Thank you, Mr. Hunter," Connie said and sat down. "How are you this morning?"

"Honestly, that depends on why you're here this time."

"Well, let's see how this goes."

"More 'routine' questions?" Quentin asked and then thought about the logic of getting smart with the FBI agent that was investigating him.

"What can you tell me about Rousseau Land Development, Mr. Hunter?" Connie asked, choosing to ignore the smart remark.

More of Daniel's shit, he thought before he answered. "Not much. I know that it is something that Daniel and Elias were involved in," Quentin said, thinking that Beason didn't answer the question of whether this investigation had anything to do with Elias being murdered. He said the two weren't related. *But the police sure think they're related.*

"And you have no involvement or investment in Rousseau Land Development?"

"Nope. After the Green Ridge project fell apart, I've had no business dealings with Daniel or Elias."

"So what you're telling me is that you didn't know that you are listed as one of the managing general partners of one of Rousseau's principle investors?"

"Wait a minute."

"A company called Innovative Strategies."

"Not Innovative Investments but Innovative Strategies?"

"That's correct. You are listed as one of its managing general partners."

"I never heard of nor do I have any involvement in Innovative Strategies, much less be one of the managing general partners."

"I see," Connie said and wrote something on the pad she brought with her. She had assumed that Innovative Strategies was no more than a shell that Quentin knew nothing about. Innovative Strategies, as well as a number of other legal filings surrounding Rousseau, were handled by Donna Smith, an attorney at Powell law firm.

"So, what are you saying?"

"That you, apparently without your knowledge or consent, are listed as one of the managing general partners of Innovative Strategies, one of Rousseau's principal investors."

"Damn right it was without my knowledge. What the fuck has Daniel gotten me involved in?"

"A scam."

"What?"

"A scam, a fraud, a hoax, a spurious imitation."

Quentin held up his hand. "I get it, Ms. Lewis."

"According to our investigation, Rousseau Land Development is a scam. New investors are shown a model of the property, which is alleged to be under development, and they are shown a virtual tour of the model house. But it's all a fraud, Mr. Hunter. There was never any construction done on the site. And the virtual tour was of the house built on the property owned by The Green Ridge Development Corporation, of which you're listed as one of the managing general partners, that was renovated for the video. Old investors were then paid with money from new investors."

Connie looked at Quentin and felt that he was actually mad and not just because she was there. She could tell by his reaction that he had no idea that any of this was going on.

"What happens now? I mean, where are you going with this?" he asked.

"Well, Mr. Hunter, I am willing to believe that you were unaware of your involvement in the Rousseau Land Development scam. However, I do recommend that you seek legal representation as soon as possible. Your involvement in that company and Green Ridge may leave you open to some criminal exposure." Connie paused and considered whether she wanted to share what else she knew about Daniel Beason. "Although it's not my duty or responsibility, I think that you should know that Mr. Beason is the main suspect in the murder of Elias Colton, and since the matter in question here involves Mr. Colton and Mr. Beason, you should protect yourself."

"Thank you, Ms. Lewis. I appreciate you giving me a heads-up on this."

"As I said, I believe that you were unaware of your involvement in Rousseau, and that is the only reason that happened," Connie said and stood up.

"And I appreciate it. Thank you again, Ms. Lewis," Quentin said and showed her out of his office. "Muthafucka!" he shouted and slammed the office door as soon as she was gone.

"What's wrong?" Samantha asked.

"That muthafuckin' Daniel got me involved in some shit again," he said as his phone rang. He looked at the display. It was Ebony calling, but he was too mad to talk to her. He sent the call to voicemail and left her a message telling her about what Connie Lewis had said and that he would confront Beason. "I promise to call you later," the message ended, but Ebony didn't like the way he sounded.

When she received the message, Ebony was in a meeting with Marvin. They were going over her plan about how she was going to buy Sataria out of the company. Seeing that the message was from Quentin, she excused herself to listen. Marvin looked on and watched Ebony's expression change as she listened to the message.

"What's wrong?" Marvin asked.

"That was Quentin Hunter," she said and began explaining the situation to him as she got ready to leave. "I don't like the way he sounded, Marvin. I'm afraid that he'll do something foolish, so I'm going over there."

"I understand. You go ahead but text me the address," he said because Ebony being involved with Quentin Hunter and him being a friend of Mike Black made this a Family matter. "I'll round up BC, and we'll meet you there."

"Thank you, Marvin," Ebony said on her way out of the office.

It was just about that same time that Jack and Diane got back to the precinct from "clearing their heads." They returned feeling refreshed and focused and ready to get back on their case.

"Jack, Diane, I'm glad you're back," Santiago said, getting up from the desk he was sitting at and coming toward them. "I got the security footage from a neighbor's camera, and it totally contradicts the statement that Beason gave you."

"Let's see it," Jack said, and they sat down.

Santiago put in the drive and cued up the footage from the neighbor's camera.

"There he is, pulling in the driveway at ten fifty-nine," Santiago said.

"That's more than enough time for him to have killed Colton and made it home," Jack stated.

"I think we got him, guys," Diane said.

"And if that's not enough to nail his ass to the cross, check this out," Santiago said and cued up another video.

"What are we looking at?" Jack asked.

"This is footage from a bank around the corner from Colton's apartment." He zoomed in. "I believe that's our guy passing by at ten minutes after ten," he said, pointing to the time stamp.

Diane took out her phone. "Who are you calling?" Jack asked.

"I'm calling Judge Peterson to get a warrant for his arrest."

Chapter Thirty-one

As she drove to Beason's house, Ebony thought about how quickly and completely she had fallen for Quentin. She didn't know if she was in love or anything like that, but she did feel something for him, and whatever it was, it was powerful enough to have her driving as fast as she could to Daniel Beason's house because she was afraid of what Quentin would do.

The problem with Quentin, if it was really a problem at all, was that he was older than her. And although she thought that was a part of why Quentin had her feeling that way regarding his maturity, it did cause her to have some reservations about him. In addition, Quentin had been married once before, and his wife left him.

And there was a reason why she left him.

She knew from experience, although limited in situations like that, that ex-wives, like ex-girlfriends, could create problems in the relationship, and in addition to the ex-wife, he did have three children in college. Ebony worried that she might not be as mature as she needed to be to deal with that. But despite those things, there were many reasons that she was excited about the possibility of a relationship with a man twenty years her senior.

It made Ebony feel good that Quentin was comfortable and secure in himself to talk freely to her about his feelings. So far, he had been a lot more attentive to her than any man that she'd been out with lately. Quentin seemed to understand what a woman likes and how she wanted and needed to be treated. It was apparent to her that he cared about her and wasn't afraid to spend time showing her rather than just saying it.

Quentin truly appreciated her *real* beauty, not just her physical beauty, which was indomitable. Through the years, he had learned to appreciate the inner beauty of a woman. So many men in her past were incapable of looking past her perceived imperfections to love her for who she truly was. His age, level of maturity, and position in life meant that he was independent and confident about his long-term plans. And there was one more plus to being in a relationship with an older man. Quentin had more experience between the sheets. He knew *exactly* what buttons to press to have her screaming and wanting more.

"What else could I ask for?" Ebony said aloud as she arrived at Daniel Beason's house.

She parked on the street behind Quentin's car and got out. Ebony noticed no vehicles in the driveway as she walked to the house and wondered if perhaps both she and Quentin had gotten there before Beason. But since Quentin wasn't standing outside waiting, she assumed that Beason's car was in the garage and pressed on toward the house.

Ebony rang the doorbell and waited awhile, but there was no answer. She rang the bell again, knocking on the door at the same time, but there was still no answer. After repeating this once more, she tried the doorknob and found that the door was unlocked. Ebony swallowed hard and stepped inside.

"Quentin," she called, and the echo reverberated throughout the empty house. "Quentin!" Ebony called again and moved slowly into the house. "Oh my God," she said when she walked into the living room and saw Quentin's body on the floor.

Ebony ran to him and dropped to her knees. "Quentin!" she shouted, shaking him, but he didn't move. That was when she saw the blood oozing from the bullet wound in his chest.

"Quentin!" she cried out, and tears flowed from her eyes as blood soaked through his shirt.

With shaking hands, Ebony took her phone from her purse and dialed 9 1 1.

"Nine-one-one operator, what is your emergency?"

At that same time outside the house, Beason pulled into his driveway. He recognized Quentin's car parked on the street and was glad that he was there. It was long past time for him to tell Quentin the truth about everything that was going on. Beason knew that if there were an investigation into Green Ridge, that sooner if not later, it would lead them to what he and Colton were doing with the proceeds from Rousseau. What was worse was that it would lead investigators down the deeper hole he was trying to climb out of.

"What is your name?" the nine-one-one operator asked.

"My name is Ebony Maddox."

"Help is on the way."

"Thank you," she said as Beason came into the living room. Ebony looked at him and backed away from the body.

"Oh my God, Quentin!" he shouted when he saw his body on the floor.

He rushed past Ebony and dropped to his knees, grabbed Quentin, and shook him.

"Oh my God—no. This can't be happening. Quentin!"

He looked up at Ebony and saw her tears and the terrified look on her face. "What happened here, Ebony?"

"You killed him—*that's* what happened," she said and began backing away when he stood up and started coming toward her.

"What?" He stopped in his tracks. "You think *I* did this?" he asked and took a step closer to her.

"Don't come any closer. The police are on the way," Ebony said with her hands out in front of her as she took another step backward.

"I didn't do this, Ebony." He looked at Quentin's body on the floor. "I couldn't," Beason said, dropping his head, and then he heard the front door open.

"Ebony," Marvin shouted. Finally, he arrived at the house with Baby Chris. "Ebony!"

"In here!" she shouted. At that moment, Beason ran out of the living room, out the back door, and made his way back around to the front of the house. He looked back to see if Marvin and Baby Chris were coming after him. Then he got into his car and drove away.

When Jack and Diane arrived to arrest Beason for Colton's murder, they found an active crime scene.

Chapter Thirty-two

Daniel Beason drove away from his house, looking in the rearview mirror. He knew that it would be the last time that he would ever see the home that he'd taken from a vacant lot of dirt, weeds, and shrubs and converted it into the seven-bedroom palace that he had envisioned all those years ago.

He thought about Susan and assumed that she'd be all right. She'd finally be free of him with more money than she knew what to do with. And with that, Susan would finally be free of the sexual prison that he had her in. Beason had lost interest in having sex with her years ago when his sexual needs and desires far exceeded Susan's willingness to participate. Beason had gotten to the point where he preferred the company of, or more to the point, the unquestioned compliance of prostitutes.

"She's better off without you," he said aloud and turned the corner.

Once again, Beason cursed himself for not disappearing in Paris when he had the chance. If he had, Quentin might still be alive.

"Fuck."

He banged on the steering wheel. This wasn't the way that things were supposed to go. Now, his two best friends were dead, and he was suspected of killing both of them. On top of that, with Colton dead, all of the trouble that Colton had brought on himself now fell on him. He thought he had taken care of the problem when he destroyed Colton's tablet, but that was just the start of his trouble. If only he hadn't lost the thumb drive, all this would be over, and then he would only have Connie Lewis to worry about.

"What the fuck am I gonna do now?" he asked as he parked in front of his office and rushed inside. Ebony had called the police, so they'd be coming, which meant that he didn't have much time. Beason hurried to his office but stopped at Andrea's first.

"My office—now," he barked before she could look up.

Beason was gone by the time she looked up. "What now?" She shook slightly and dropped her head before she got up.

When she got to his office, Andrea found Beason in front of his safe, frantically searching through the documents for the ones he needed. Although cleaning up the mess that Colton had gotten him into was the more pressing issue at the moment, especially now that Quentin was dead, and Ebony would undoubtedly tell the police that he killed him, Connie Lewis would eventually uncover what he and Colton were doing with Rousseau. He needed to protect Susan from as much liability as he could. Although he cheated on her, he loved Susan. She had nothing to do with what he had done, so there was no reason for her to take the weight.

"The police were here again. They think that you killed Elias," Andrea said as she walked in.

"I know," he said and kept shuffling through documents. "They think that I killed Quentin too."

"Quentin's dead?"

"Somebody shot him in my house."

Andrea looked at him. She had worked for Beason for the last five years and knew that he had no problem walking the line between legal and illegal, but until that second, she didn't think he was capable of murder.

"In your house?" she asked skeptically. "What was Quentin doing at your house?"

"I don't know." He turned around and saw how Andrea was looking at him. "He was there when I got there, and he was already dead."

"What are you doing?"

"I need to get out of the country," he said and handed the documents to her. "Try to straighten out—" he began to tell her what was going on. After all, Andrea did have his complete confidence, but

Beason knew that the less she knew about what he and Colton were involved in, the better that it would be for her. "I need you to destroy these and call Donna. Tell her that she needs to get rid of anything that leads to Rousseau." He closed the safe. "And you should do the same," Beason said, not knowing that she and Donna Smith had already taken steps to insulate themselves from Connie Lewis's investigation.

"Where are you going to go, Daniel?"

"I told you, I gotta get out of the country for a while. I need to get to the Turks and Caicos to clear my name." He stopped and looked at her. "I'm sorry I got you into this mess, Andrea."

I am too. Regardless of whether she liked it, she knew she needed to do everything that she could to help Beason. Although she had taken steps to insulate herself, the conversation she had with Connie Lewis did not go well, and it told her that she was in grave danger of facing bank fraud charges. Helping Beason might be the only way to protect herself. "How are you going to get out of the country if the police are looking for you? Won't they have the airport covered or something like that?"

"I'll figure it out," he said and started for the door.

"Wait!"

"What?"

Andrea exhaled and collected herself. "I know somebody that owns a jet, and I've gotten to be good friends with his pilot. I can get him to fly you to the Turks and Caicos, but it will cost you."

Thinking that the police would, if they hadn't already, flag his passport, Beason thought for a moment and decided that it would be safer for him, no matter what the cost.

"How much?"

When she got off the phone, she told him the price. "Fifteen thousand."

Beason went back to the safe and opened it. He reached in and came out with two stacks of bills.

"That's twenty, but can you call him on the way. I gotta get outta here now. The police will be coming if they're not already on their way," Beason said. They left the office, and Andrea made the call on the way to her car.

With the deal set, once they got to the parking lot, she told him to get in the trunk so no one would see him, and she would drive him to the private airfield where the jet would be waiting. Beason climbed into the trunk of her seven-series BMW and tried to get as comfortable as he could for the ride to the airport. Once he arrived at the Turks and Caicos Islands, he would make it to Colton's bungalow and hope that he could find what he needed. It took over an hour before the car stopped, and Beason heard the trunk latch release.

"Help him out," Beason heard a voice he knew say . . . and he realized that he was in worse trouble than when he got into the trunk.

When the two men helped Beason out of the trunk, he saw that he was not in an airport hangar where a private jet was waiting to take him to the Turks and Caicos but in a warehouse. Lendina Neziri, the "*mik*" of the Troka Clan, an Albanian mafia organization, was holding a gun to Andrea's head.

"I'm sorry, Daniel. They were there as soon as I closed the trunk," she said with tears staining her makeup as it rolled down her cheeks.

"Where is it?" Neziri asked.

"I don't have it. I was about to go to the Turks and Caicos to see if I could find the backup copy."

"You were trying to leave the country," Neziri said and shot Andrea in the head.

All that Beason could do was drop his head and look away in disgust at the damage that both he and Colton were responsible for. If only Colton had listened, none of this would be happening. Beason had done everything that he could to stop this from occurring. These were dangerous people Colton had got them involved with. For a while, things were going well and would soon get to the point where they would get out of the red and begin to see a profit . . . and then Neziri came to see him on the day Colton was killed.

"We have a serious problem," Neziri began. As mik or friend of The Kryetar or boss of the clan, he was responsible for coordinating the clan's activities. That night, it meant he was cleaning up behind Saemira Vetone. "Mr. Colton has come into possession of some information that needs to be returned as soon as possible before things begin to happen that are not part of my control."

"What kind of information?"

"The kind that gets people killed," Neziri warned.

That evening, Beason went to see Colton to find out what information Neziri was talking about. But Colton was expecting Gayle Eager to arrive, so they went to a bar nearby and had a drink.

"What is Neziri talking about? What information?"

"Call it 'insurance.'"

"'Insurance'? What kind of insurance?"

"That's all you need to know right now."

"Come on, Elias, what is it?"

"It's something that's going to protect us in the future. Trust me, you'll see. With the information that I now have in my possession, we are in a much stronger position, and that is a good thing, right?" he said and paused. "You leave Neziri to me. I'll give him a call this evening and straighten out the whole thing."

"You sure you know what you're doing?"

"Always," Colton said and shot his drink. "Gotta go, buddy. Don't want to keep Mrs. Eager waiting."

And he thought that was the end of it. Colton would straighten everything out, and it would be fine. So he left the bar and returned to his office for his meeting with Andrea. However, later that evening, before he left the office, Beason got a video from Neziri.

It began with Neziri sitting in his car with one finger over his lips. Then the video cut to a shot of him walking through Beason's house and into the bedroom. As he stood over Susan, who was asleep in bed, Neziri put one finger over his lips again, pulled a knife with a serrated edge from behind his back, and raised it. After that, the video cuts back to him sitting in his car.

"I thought that I made myself clear. I want back what Colton stole from Saemira Vetone," Neziri said, and the video ended.

Knowing that Neziri would make good on his threat of killing Susan, Beason left his office and drove to Colton's apartment as fast as possible. Fortunately, Gayle was gone when he got there. They had a drink, and he pleaded with his friend to return what he had taken from Neziri.

"First of all, I didn't steal anything from Saemira Vetone. The information I have was given to me freely," Colton said and tapped on his tablet.

"What difference does it make?" Beason asked as there was a knock at the door, and Colton got up to answer. "He was *in* my house."

"Send Susan on vacation to Hawaii for a couple of weeks with her mother and her annoying-ass sisters until this blows over," Colton said and opened the door.

"Hello, Elias," Neziri said with his gun in Colton's face as he backed him into the apartment. Beason jumped up from the couch. "You know what I came for. Get it."

"Okay, okay," Colton said. He led Neziri to the office. It was less than a minute later when Beason heard the sounds of a struggle and rushed into the room in time to see the two men crash through the glass door out on the balcony. Beason rushed out to try to separate them, but it was too late.

Neziri turned quickly, pulled out his gun, and pointed it in Beason's face. "I want back what Colton stole from Saemira Vetone," he said and left the apartment.

Beason rushed out of the apartment but knowing that what Neziri was looking for was on Colton's tablet, he went back for it. He also took the glasses that he and Colton were drinking from, washed, and put them away before he left. He planned to copy the data to a thumb drive, destroy the tablet in Paris, and turn over the information to Bujare Fazliu, Neziri's associate in Switzerland.

However, when it came time to hand off the information, Beason couldn't find it.

He frantically searched his pockets, sure that he'd put the drive into his pocket right after he copied it to the drive. That was when he thought about Paige and how distracted he was when she shook her big tits in his face. Beason looked up at Neziri and knew that he wouldn't hesitate to kill him.

"Where is it?"

"I must have dropped it on the plane."

Neziri didn't believe what Beason had said about the drive, so he called Executive Flight Lines to inquire if perhaps a flight attendant had turned it in, but the person he spoke to apologized and advised Neziri that no one had turned in anything that day.

After that, Neziri dispatched Ismail Flamur to search the apartment of the flight attendant that they believed found it, but not only couldn't he find it but he was also interrupted in his search by Rain Robinson.

Neziri slowly walked toward Beason and put the barrel of his gun to Beason's forehead. "I'm going to ask you one more time—where is it?"

"I told you that I don't have it. But there's a backup copy at Elias's place in the Turks and

Caicos. That's where I was going, and she was helping get out of the country." He looked at Andrea's body. "You didn't have to kill her."

"Get it. Or your wife and her family are next."

Neziri left Beason in the warehouse looking at Andrea's body.

Chapter Thirty-three

"Sorry, Rain, but I guess she ain't nowhere to be found. But I'll stay on it."

As promised, Carla was as good as her word. She was able to tell Rain that Overseas Air was a front company for an Albanian mafia organization called the Troka Clan that was involved in the international trafficking of organs. Also known as The Red Market, the trading of human organs, tissues, or other body products generates profits between six hundred million and one point six billion dollars per year.

"Which makes you wonder, was she an escort or a flight attendant like her mother said?" was the question that Carla asked, and Rain had no answer for it. But that was the same answer with everything about this.

And there were a lot of unanswered questions.

If Fire was an escort, what would she have to do with Overseas Air?

And if she were a flight attendant, why Overseas Air?

What was somebody looking for in her apartment?

Was the person who searched the apartment and attacked her involved with Overseas Air?

Or was Vonetta right that Fire had nothing to do with them because they were bad news?

Those were all questions that Rain had asked. If she found out the answer to those questions, maybe then she would have an answer to the bigger questions: where was Fire, what were they looking for, and who were they?

So Rain was back in Fire's apartment, looking through the mess, trying to find an answer to those unanswered questions, when she heard the door open and the distinct sound of heels against a hardwood floor.

"What the fuck?"

She looked around her apartment and was shocked to see that her furniture was turned over, pillow cushions cut open, their fillings emptied onto the floor. The place was a mess—and then she saw somebody. Rain drew her gun and pointed it at the woman dressed in a flight attendant outfit. "Who the fuck are you?"

"Who the fuck are *you?*" she shouted. This wasn't the first time she'd had a gun pointed at her.

"I'm the one with the gun."

"I live here."

"You're Fire Langston?" Rain asked and lowered her gun.

"Sapphire, but, yes. Now, who the fuck are you?"

"I'm your cousin. Your mother and my mother were sisters."

"Lorraine?"

"Rain, but, yeah."

Sapphire's eyes opened wide. "Robinson?"

"Yeah."

"You're Rain Robinson, and you're my cousin?"

"Yeah."

"Now, you can tell me what the fuck you're doing in my apartment and what are you're looking for?"

"I'm looking for you. Your mother is worried about you."

"And she called you?" Sapphire asked and wondered why her mother never mentioned that Rain Robinson was her cousin.

"No. She told Millie, and Millie told me. I promised your mother I would look for you." Rain paused. "But I had nothing to do with all this."

"Well, who did?" she asked angrily, walking through her apartment looking at the destruction.

"*You* tell me. Somebody is looking for something, and whatever it is, they are willing to kill for it."

Sapphire stopped. "What? Kill for it?"

Rain nodded. "Come here," she said and led Sapphire to the wall. "Those are the bullet holes from where the guy that was searching your apartment tried to kill me."

Sapphire looked at Rain, shocked at what she had just heard and was unable to speak.

"So, *you* tell *me,* what would somebody be looking for?" she asked, but Sapphire didn't answer.

Unknown to Rain and Sapphire, three men had been watching the apartment waiting for her to return. Once they saw Sapphire go in, the men exited their vehicle and entered the building one at a time so they wouldn't draw attention to themselves.

"Sapphire," Rain said to snap her out of her thoughts, "you all right?"

"No. I come home, and my place is trashed. Then you tell me that somebody might be trying to kill me over something I know nothing about. No, I'm *not* all right," Sapphire said as the apartment door suddenly burst open.

"Run!" Rain yelled as two men rushed in and opened fire.

Sapphire ran into the bedroom as Rain reached for her gun and returned their fire. While she shot it out with the first two men, a third man entered the apartment and went after Sapphire in the bedroom. Rain fired and hit the first man that came through the door. When he went down from a shot to the chest, Rain opened fire on the second shooter. Her first two shots were accurate and found their mark. Once Rain had dispensed with them, she ran into the bedroom and found the third man with his gun to Sapphire's head.

"Drop it!" he shouted and pressed the gun against her temple. "I'll kill her. Just give us what we came for, and nobody has to die."

But instead of dropping her gun, Rain fired and hit him with one shot right between the eyes.

"Are you fuckin' crazy?" Sapphire shouted.

"No, I'm a good shot." Rain grabbed her by the hand. "Come on. We gotta go."

"Where are we going?"

"Someplace where you'll be safe until I figure this out."

Sapphire grabbed her suitcase and followed Rain out of the apartment.

They bypassed the elevator and took the stairs down to the lobby. Just in case there were more men in the lobby waiting for them, Rain called Alwan and told him to meet her in the lobby on the way down.

"What happened?" Alwan asked as he got out of the car and rushed toward the building.

"Three men just tried to kill us."

"Us?"

"Sapphire is with me, and we're coming down the stairs," Rain said as Alwan entered the building.

"Lobby is clear."

Once they were out of the building, Sapphire got the rest of her luggage from her car, and they drove away from there.

"Where to?" Alwan asked.

"Take us back to Wanda's safe house."

"Safe house?" Sapphire questioned.

"So you'll be safe," Alwan said as he drove on.

When they got to the house, Alwan brought in her luggage while Rain showed Sapphire around Wanda's house and told her where everything was. Once she got her cousin settled, Rain left her alone to calm her shattered nerves. As she lay there, stretched across the bed, Sapphire could not believe that somebody wanted to kill her. The part that bothered her most was that she had no idea what they wanted with her and why. But in the mix of all that, there was one other thing that was blowing Sapphire.

"You're Rain Robinson," Sapphire said, standing in Rain's doorway.

She nodded.

"Rain Robinson . . . my cousin. Wow. Mommy never mentioned that," she said as she drifted slowly into Rain's room.

"I don't think she knew."

"My cousin." She shook her head.

"Did you call your mother?"

"I did."

"She said you'd have some fantastic story about where you been." Rain sat up in bed. "So, cousin, where the fuck you been? I was starting to think your ass was dead. I had some of the best trackers in the world looking for your ass, and neither one of them could find you."

When Carla struck out looking for Sapphire, Monika called her an amateur, but she had to apologize when she couldn't find her either.

"I was on a fourteen-day Mediterranean cruise."

"You're kidding."

"The tour started from Rome and visited Venice, the Greek Isles, Croatia, Barcelona, Marseille, and then back to Rome."

"My girls must be slipping."

Sapphire laughed. "They were probably looking for Sapphire Langston."

"Ah—yeah."

Sapphire shook her head. "Who they should have been looking for is Penelope Pits."

"The fuck is Penelope Pits?"

"Me," Sapphire smiled.

"Okay, you gonna have to walk me through that one."

"Penelope Pitstop was a character in a cartoon called The Perils of Penelope Pitstop. It was my mother's favorite cartoon when she was a little girl, and we used to watch the videos together. Penelope used to wear this cute pink outfit, and the name of her car was the Compact Pussycat. She used to travel all over the world . . . *the Glamour Gal of the Gas Pedal*," she giggled. "Anyway, when I had a chance to get some fake documents, including a passport, that was the name I used. So now, when I travel for pleasure, that's the name I use. Sounds silly, right?"

"A little, but it's kind of cute," Rain laughed, but she was a little jealous because she never got to share anything with her mother. "But it does explain why they couldn't' find you." Rain paused. "Mind if I ask you another question?"

"Go ahead."

"Are you a flight attendant or an escort?"

Sapphire smiled. "You know, as soon as you called me Fire, I knew that you had been talking to Vonee." She paused. "I'm a flight attendant-turned-escort-turned-flight attendant."

"There's a story to this; gotta be."

"There is." Sapphire made herself comfortable on Rain's bed. "So I'm at a girlfriend's wedding, and the reception is in a hotel ballroom. After the reception, I stopped at the bar for a drink, and I met this man. He's nice, good-looking. I'm a little drunk and very horny, so up to a room, we go. When we're done, and he gets ready to leave, he says, 'You never said what your rate was, so I hope a thousand will cover it,' and he leaves. A thousand dollars, and he barely lasted fifteen minutes."

"Easy money."

"I was back the next night, and that's when I met Vonee. She was working that bar and brought me to her agency." Sapphire shrugged her shoulders. "And for a little while, I made that money. But after a while, I knew that wasn't me, so I quit and got a job with a small private airline."

"So why does your girl still think you're an escort?"

"When I told her I was quitting, she tried to talk me out of it, and to shut her up, I told her that I was just going independent." Sapphire's eyes suddenly opened wide. "You didn't say anything about me being an escort to my mother, did you?"

"No," Rain laughed.

"Good. *That* is a conversation I *never* want to have with her."

"Your secret's safe with me."

"I'm going to call it a night." Sapphire stood up. "And, Rain . . . Thanks for saving my life tonight."

"See you in the morning. Then we'll figure out who is after you and why."

Chapter Thirty-four

After she gave her statement to the police on the scene, Ebony was permitted to leave Daniel Beason's house, and since Marvin didn't think that she should drive, she rode with him, and Baby Chris drove her car home.

Although Ebony hadn't known Quentin for very long, his death hit her hard. Alone in her room, she cried and thought about what might have been. Could he have become her lifelong partner, someone she could share her deepest secrets with, someone she could count on to stand by her when things got hard?

It took a couple of days before Ebony felt like she was ready to be interviewed by the police. Although she was a lawyer and didn't need one, Marvin didn't want her to be alone. With that thought in mind, he spoke with Patrick Freeman, the managing general partner at Wanda Moore and Associates, The Family's law firm. He assigned his best criminal defense attorney, Akilah

Malheiros, to go with Ebony for support. They'd
met years ago at Nick's wedding, they were two
young lawyers working for the same company, so
they clicked. They'd hung out a few times, so it was
all good, and Akilah was glad to do it.

"Ms. Maddox," Jack said when he and Diane
came into the room, "I'm Detective Harmon, and
this is Detective Mitchell. Thank you for coming in
to talk to us."

"Detectives, this is my friend and attorney,
Akilah Malheiros."

Akilah put up her hands. "I'm just here for support."

"But you have no firsthand knowledge of the
case?" Diane asked.

"I do not," Akilah said.

"Well, let's get started, Ms. Maddox," Jack began.
"Can you tell me what happened the day that Mr.
Hunter was murdered?"

"Earlier that day, I got a message from Mr.
Hunter. He said that he had spoken with Special
Agent Connie Lewis of the FBI about a business
deal that he was supposedly involved in with Mr.
Beason, and he was going to confront him about it."

"Do you know what the nature of that business
was between them?" Jack asked for confirmation
since they had spoken with Connie Lewis, and she

shared some preliminary information about the case.

"Yes. Quentin told me that Beason had proposed that he and Elias Colton buy 230 acres of undeveloped land to subdivide the site into vacation homes. As a result, the Green Ridge Development Corporation was formed, but he said that when interest rates rose, the venture failed."

"I realize that it was just a brief message," Diane began, "but how would you characterize his mood after hearing about his possible criminal exposure in that case?"

"Quentin was mad. I hadn't known him that long, but I know how mad he was about that situation."

"How so?" Diane asked.

"We had talked about the situation between him and Mr. Beason when he first heard about it. He told me about how prior business between them had gone in the past, and I heard that same type of anger in his voice. The two of them had been good friends for years, so part of his anger was Quentin, excuse me, Mr. Hunter, feeling Mr. Beason had betrayed the friendship."

Diane leaned back. "Betrayal is a very powerful emotion."

"So Mr. Hunter leaves you an angry message. What happened after that?" Jack asked.

"I didn't like the way he sounded, so I went to Mr. Beason's house. When I got there, Mr. Hunter was dead, so I called the police. That was when Mr. Beason came into the room."

"You told the officers that when you got there that Mr. Hunter's car was parked on the street, but you didn't see Mr. Beason's, is that correct?" Jack asked.

"Yes."

"Could the car have been in the garage and he have been someplace else in the house?" Diane wanted to know.

"I don't know. The car could have been in the garage, but I don't know. All that I can tell you is that he said that he didn't do it, and then he ran out the back door."

"When you arrived at the house, did you see any other cars leaving the area?" Diane asked. She could feel the pain that Ebony was in.

"No, I didn't see any other cars leaving when I got there."

As Jack asked Ebony questions about what happened when Beason arrived, Diane looked at him and wondered how she'd feel if something happened to him. And what would she do? Diane was a woman with a badge and a gun—and that made her dangerous.

"He ran past me, and then he dropped to his knees and shook Quentin. He said, 'Oh my God—no. This can't be happening.'"

"What happened next?" Jack asked.

"He said he didn't do it and ran out of there," Ebony said. After a few more questions, Jack and Diane stood up and thanked her for her time.

"I'm very sorry for your loss," Diane said as they left the room.

The detectives' next stop was the home of Daniel Beason to speak with his wife, Susan. Once they arrived at the house, Jack and Diane found the driveway filled with cars with license plates from Massachusetts, Pennsylvania, and Georgia. When they rang the bell, a tall, lanky teenager with a bad case of acne opened the door.

"What y'all want?"

"We're here to see Susan Beason," Jack said.

"Who the fuck are you?" he boldly asked.

Jack and Diane looked at each other and then at the young man . . . and then shoved their badges in his face.

"We're the police," Diane said. "So why don't we try this again so that I don't have to kick your young, disrespectful ass, okay?"

The teen quickly nodded as Jack tried to keep a stone face.

"Good boy." She patted his cheek. "We're here to see Susan Beason."

"Come in," he said and let them into the house.

"Who are you?" Jack asked as the teen led them through the house.

"I'm Wesley."

"And you are?"

"I'm Aunt Susan's nephew."

With a new attitude in place, he led the detectives through the living room and out onto the deck. There, they found Susan, surrounded by her mother and her two sisters. They each arrived the night before to offer moral support and to see and hear the latest firsthand. As they approached, the detectives found the four women sitting around the pool enjoying drinks, and the mood seemed celebratory. And why shouldn't it be? Beason was right. Susan would be better off without him, and she knew it, and so did her family. Susan was glad that he was gone and hoped he didn't come back. Now, she could live her life on her own terms and not inside the perfect wife box that her husband had carefully crafted and placed her in.

"Who was at the door, Wesley?" Susan's mother asked.

"The police, Grandma," Wesley said and turned to go back into the house.

Diane stopped Wesley before he made it inside. "Don't forget what I said about kicking your young, disrespectful ass."

"Yes, ma'am—I mean, no, ma'am, I won't forget," he said and rushed into the house.

"What can I do for you, Detectives?" Susan asked.

"We're sorry to bother you, Mrs. Beason, but we need to ask you some questions," Jack said.

Susan finished her drink, put down the glass, and stood up wearing Givenchy Logo banded crop top and leggings, and from Jack's point of view, she was wearing it *very* well.

"Let's talk inside," she said. "Excuse me, ladies. I'm sure this won't take long," Susan said and started walking toward the house with Jack and Diane following behind her.

Once inside, Susan went into the kitchen, and they sat down at the table. "What can I do for you?"

"When was the last time that you saw or spoke with your husband?" Jack asked.

"The night that you were here."

"What did you tell him?" he asked.

"I told him that you had been here and that you were asking questions about his alibi and that you made it seem like he was a suspect in Elias's murder," she replied.

"What did he say?" Diane asked.

"He didn't say anything. He left. He didn't say another word. He just left."

"What can you tell me about the business that your husband had with Mr. Colton?"

"Nothing. I can't tell you a thing about Danny's business with Elias or anybody else." She dropped her head, and a look of regret washed over her. Then she looked up and turned to Diane. "You see, Detective, I wasn't my husband's partner. I was his property, or at least that's how he made me feel. Although I hate the stereotype, I was his trophy wife."

Diane shook her head. She'd known women like Susan, young and attractive, married to an older, more powerful man whose role in the relationship was to provide her with power and material wealth, which Beason did in abundance.

"Do you have any idea where we might find Mr. Beason?" Jack asked.

"I really don't." Susan paused. "And honestly, I don't care. Knowing Danny, he's probably out of the country by now on one of his hooker flights."

"Hooker flights?" Diane questioned.

"That's what I call the airline he always uses when he travels. It's called Executive Flight Lines."

"I see," Diane said, smiling and standing up. "I think that's all we need, for now, Mrs. Beason."

"If you think of anything, please call me," Jack said, and the detectives left the house no closer to catching up to Beason or finding out what any of this was about.

"What now?" Diane asked.

"I think we should check out Executive Flight Lines, and then we need to see what we can dig up on The Green Ridge Development Corporation and Rousseau Land Development. After that, we need to talk to Connie Lewis. Maybe then we can get our heads around a motive." Jack chuckled. "Since the motive isn't your usual sex and money."

"Not going to let me live that down, are you, Jack?"

"Not for a long time, Diane. Not for a long time."

Chapter Thirty-five

The following day, Quentin Hunter was laid to rest at Saint Luke's Episcopal Church. In attendance was Quentin's first wife, Leslie, and their children, Joseph and Georgia Connor, Albert Eager, and those who knew were surprised that Gayle was with him. Elaine Cargill and her husband, Walter, were there as well. Colton's wife, Cissy, was there, as was Susan Beason, her mother, and two sisters.

Ebony sat in the front row. Marvin was sitting next to her, and her coworkers from Pearson MDS Construction, Dominica Paris and Ramel Quincy, were there with her, and Mr. and Mrs. Black were seated in the row behind them.

"I did not know Quentin on the same level as many of you knew him. From all accounts, however, Quentin Hunter was an extraordinary individual. To some, he was a father; to others, a husband, a colleague, or a friend. To God, he is a beloved child. There is a sense in which the death of any person who bears God's image is a tragedy. When Jesus came to the funeral of his friend Lazarus, Jesus wept. Jesus knew better than anyone that Lazarus would soon be resuscitated and ultimately resurrected, but nevertheless, the death of his friend caused our Lord to weep. The Apostle Paul tells us in Philippians, chapter one, 'For to me to live is Christ, and to die is gain. If I am to live in the flesh, that means fruitful labor for me. Yet which I shall choose I cannot tell. I am hard-pressed between the two. My desire is to depart and be with Christ, for that is far better,'" Father Went read at the celebration of the life of Quentin Hunter.

After the service concluded, Black spoke to Ebony for a while to see that she was all right. Then he escorted Shy to the Mercedes parked outside of Saint Luke's Episcopal Church.

"There are your cop friends," Shy said as they walked. Black turned to see Jack and Diane leaning against a car parked across the street. He nodded to acknowledge their presence before he opened Shy's door and then got in. Chuck took them to the house.

"I'm surprised they didn't want to talk to you," Shy said as they rode to New Rochelle.

"I'm not. They never did think I did it."

"Then what did they want to talk to you about?"

"Detective Mitchell wants me to be a murder consultant for her," Black said and looked out the window. He had a lot on his mind.

"A murder consultant?"

"Yeah, a murder consultant." He looked at his wife and smiled. "She said that I know more about murder than either of them."

"She *really* said that?"

"She did."

"Well, I guess it's true," she giggled. "Especially with your history of violence."

"Yeah," he said and looked out the window.

"What's wrong, Michael?"

"Just thinking."

"What about?"

"Thinking about what Daniel and Elias could have been into." He paused. "Whatever it was, it was enough to get Quentin killed and for Andrea to disappear."

"Andrea's missing?"

"Nobody's seen her since the day Quentin was murdered."

Shy looked at Black. She'd seen that look before. "You're going to find out who killed him, aren't you?"

He smiled at Shy. "You know me too well, my love."

Later that night, Black and Bobby were in the basement of Bobby's house waiting for Wanda to arrive. He asked her to meet them there so they could talk about something important.

"Without my knowledge, Rain, Jackie, Carter, and a few others were involved in the murder of Greg Mac and Drum for Gavin Caldwell," Black said.

"How'd you find out?" Bobby asked.

"Angelo put me on to it, and Jackie told me the details. But neither of them should have told me. This was something that I needed to hear from her."

"You're right. She should have told you," Wanda said. "You shouldn't have had to hear that from Jackie."

Bobby shot his drink. "I agree, but I can understand why she would think that you would be cool with it. You and she backed Vince when he had a problem," he said because he made the same mistake when he chose to back Leon against Rico, and The Family got dragged into their drug war, someplace where Black never wanted to be and wished to avoid.

"I understand that too, Bob, but if she thought it was cool, why didn't she tell me about it?"

"He's right, Bobby. There is no reason for her not to tell him." She turned to Black. "Have you talked to her about it?"

"Not yet."

"Are you going to?" she asked.

"Or you gonna put her through one of your damn tests to test her judgment?" Bobby asked.

"You know, Bob, that's not a bad idea," Black said and got up to pour another drink.

"By the way, Mike, I was sorry to hear about Quentin," Wanda said.

"Thanks, Wanda."

"Have the police found Beason yet?" she asked.

"No, they haven't, but Ebony doesn't think he did it," Black said and looked at Bobby. "I was thinking about, you know, asking a few questions."

"You want some company?" Bobby asked.

Black smiled. "Always."

"Oh no," Wanda said and sipped her Apple Martini. "The two of you . . . back in the streets."

"Don't call it a comeback," Bobby said and fist-bumped Black.